LEAD AND ROSES

LOVE SONGS AT THE END OF THE WORLD

NATALIE IRONSIDE

LEAD AND ROSES

LOVE SONGS AT THE END OF THE WORLD

NATALIE IRONSIDE

CONTENTS

GNU Sara Blackwood
May her memory be a blessing

The wasteland is not a kind place. The stories in this collection are stories of hope, but of hope in defiance of despair. It was my intention to treat the grimmer aspects of life in the wasteland with appropriate tact, rather than as salacious spectacle, but racism, transphobia, sexual violence, messy recoveries, and—of course—good old violence and bloodshed are themes throughout. Forewarned is forearmed.

ARGUMENT

The five short stories in this collection—two slice-of-life stories, two horror stories, and one military adventure story-- were written during the bleaked years of 2020 and 2021 as a way to temporarily stave off madness while pondering the setting and characters of my novel, *The Last Girl Scout*. All five stories take place within the universe of *The Last Girl Scout*, either a few generations before or a couple of years after the novel's main plot, and I've intended *Lead and Roses* to be a little follow-up or companion piece to that six-hundred-page leviathan (available wherever fine books are sold!), but I believe any reader can enjoy them without having read all of that beautiful door-stopper. For accessibility's sake I will provide a brief outline of important events and key characters along with a brief description of each story at the end of this little diatribe, but I hope that that is not strictly-speaking necessary.

This fun little world I've made up grew out of a life-long obsession with dystopian, post-apocalyptic, and survivalist media; I think that fans of the *S.T.A.L.K.E.R.* video game franchise, George Miller's *Mad Max* tetralogy, or George Romero's zombie films will find a lot to love in here, if only because they're probably the same kind of nerd that I am. And, as a life-long fan of the genre, I've been constantly frustrated by the way so many of my favorite works seem to revel in futility, hopelessness, and the worst parts of humanity. In my experience throughout my very strange and poorly-thought-out life and through the many adventures that were forced upon me against my will, life gives us innumerable opportunities to be at our best when the world around us is at its worst. Dystopia is a genre that's meant to rail against the status quo, and when the order of the day is despair, the only true rebellion is hope.

The world of *The Last Girl Scout* is a grim future where humanity dwells on small islands of civilization amongst vast oceans of death, where death is an ever-present part of life and where an existence worth living in rests on a knife's edge, often literally; "Where the climate is raw and the gun makes the law," as the late Bobby Sands said. But the heroes of these stories are those rebels who've forged those small islands of civilization by choosing to rail against the darkness and believe, like true renegades, that the world can always be a better place.

As you read my silly little tales, I hope you enjoy reading them half as much as I enjoyed writing them, and I hope that you, like the heroes of my stories, can find the courage to believe in a future that's worth fighting for.

In love and solidarity,

Natalie H. Ironside
Horror Writers Association
IWW Freelance Journalists Union

In the 2060s, civilization as we know it was brought to a screeching, violent halt and the world was forever changed by a global thermonuclear and biological warfare exchange between several world powers. As the remnants of humanity learned how to survive in this new world, the societies they built followed two divergent paths: Some sought to build a better world, while others sought to reclaim the glory of Old America.

In southern Appalachia in the 2180s, a group of settlements threatened by encroaching warlords banded together to form the Free Appalachian Army under the leadership of two women from Tennessee, Laurelei Bluecrow and Maxine Mondragon Reyez. After defeating two warlord armies—the Black Army Volunteers of Commander Ragnar Rockwell and the United Christian Army of Father Murphy Covington—

and forcing them north of the Ohio River by the year 2191, the Free Appalachian Army disbanded and formed the Ashland Confederated Republic, made up of three cantons and one anarchist autonomous zone. Conversely, the two warlords and the remnants of their armies joined forces to form the autocratic Blackland New Republic north of the river. The ACR and BNR would then be locked in a bloody stalemate with occasional border skirmishes for the next 70 years until, in the year 2261, a series of events (the main plot of *The Last Girl Scout*) led to the collapse of the BNR and the opening up of previously little-explored parts of the wasteland. Two key players in those events were Magnolia Blackadder, an ACR political commissar, and Julia Binachi, a former BNR stormtrooper who defected to the Ashlanders' side following years of unspeakable abuse and seeks to make amends for her deeply troubled past.

Lead and Roses contains the following tales, arranged thematically rather than chronologically:

Stories: Two women stand on the edge of oblivion and dare o believe in a future.

The Last American: A red star is rising over southern Appalachia, and one man has the courage to remain true to God and embody the spirit of Old America against the godless communist hordes. It goes about as well for him as you'd expect.

The White Goddess: A group of scientists set out to explore the wasteland and come face-to-face with the pernicious refusal of the past to die.

Werewolf: A boy who became a stormtrooper chasing dreams of heroism discovers that being a man of action doesn't quite live up to expectations.

That's a Christmas to Me: A woman struggling with her faith, her identity, and her dark and troubled past finds some small shred of redemption and learns an important lesson about motorcycle safety. (Originally published as a Patreon exclusive for the 2020 winter holiday season)

1: STORIES

[AD 2191, 126 years post-War; Kentucky]

LAURI WASN'T BUILT FOR WAR, AT LEAST NOT THE WAY Max was, but she'd taken to war the way she took to everything else: Fighting, but fully and all the way.

Max would always remember the day they first met, all those years ago when she first saw Laurelei Bluecrow, the small, timid girl with that rich black hair she conditioned with sumac berries, wearing a blue gingham dress, carrying a long rifle under her arm and a baby in a sling on her back, surveying the world with iron determination in those big, sad eyes. Max had fallen in love with her right off, she was so beautiful. And she still had those same eyes; wells of fire and hope and a deep, bottomless sadness.

Come to think of it, that was how Lauri had come to womanhood as well: Fighting, but fully and all the way.

And Lauri, tiny Lauri, nervous and soft-spoken Lauri who began every sentence with "excuse me" and studied her boots wherever she walked, was not the one that anyone expected to become a bandit chief, leader of an army, leader of several armies, builder of a nation; everyone who knew her had expected to her to spend her whole life in her grandmama's cabin south of Roan Mountain, raising chickens, feeding orphans, and scribbling in the notebooks she always carried around. But there was something in those books that Lauri surrounded herself with. Maxine Reyez was the soldier, and when she commanded, people obeyed; but Lauri . . . Little Lauri Bluecrow had big dreams, and when she spoke about them, people listened. And when the war finally came, Max may have been the one the people followed, but Lauri was the one they listened to.

Max's old uncle Bernardo, who'd first introduced little Lauri to names like Lenin and Trotsky and Feinberg and Bookchin a million years ago when they were both just little girls, used to joke that the two women together made one whole revolutionary.

Max had known that she was born to live by the sword from the very first time Bernardo put a gun in her hand and took her with him on a run towards the coast to look for computer parts, and when they ran into those bandits around what was left of Richmond—close enough to the exclusion zone around Old DC to see the fireworks of ionizing radiation in the air whenever a storm blew in off the Atlantic—and she learned what it meant to kill a man. She was the soldier, but Bernardo had always said that a soldier without idealism is just another bandit, and sweet little Lauri had enough idealism to build a nation with.

Not that she would've ever called it that. Lauri Bluecrow could be real particular about which words meant what, and if anyone had said that, she probably would've mumbled, "Um, excuse me, but I'm not an idealist, I'm a materialist."

And when the survivalists and the Jesus-freaks and the petty warlords and the last of the Old Americans and other sorts of no-goods and no-accounts who were ruining a perfectly good post-nuclear wasteland and still dreaming of Old America started banding together to make more trouble, well, they weren't exactly *ready*, but they knew what to do. And towns came together to make federations, and town militias came together to make flying columns, and columns came together to make the Free Appalachian Army. Bernardo always said that iron with guts behind it could accomplish anything, but only if there was a will behind that, and Max figured that that was what happened when the war really picked up and she and Lauri finally got married under the hawthorn tree outside of Old Maggie Bluecrow's cabin near Roan Mountain; iron and guts had found its will.

And it was a long, hard war and a dirty war, and they buried a lot of friends, and a lot of the towns they'd once federated with didn't exist anymore, and they all bore deep, ugly scars inside and out, just like the land that bore them, just like the land they fought on. And toward the end, when they'd really started to win, banditry became something else, or maybe became what it had always really been; fasces and swastikas could be spotted in among the Confederate and of course American flags on the opposing lines. But that had been toward the end, and the end was over now, or at least over enough for them to be getting on with.

And after six years of bloody war and bitter struggle, the last enemy stronghold on their side of the river had fallen that morning. The belt of settlements along the Ohio Valley had gone down like a row of dominoes, none of the residents feeling particularly patriotic about the warlords who claimed ownership of them, and that played out as well when they attacked the star fort near Maysville, the last stronghold of Old America and last enemy staging point south of the Ohio River. It went the usual way—bombardment by mobile mortar teams in the beds of trucks followed by Max leading an infantry assault—but when they made it over the parapet the garrison surrendered en mass. Which is to be expected when your enemy fields conscripts and mercenaries.

And so there was peace, or something approximating peace, near enough to peace, from the Ohio River in the north to the bombed-out and irradiated ruins of Atlanta and Birmingham in the south, from the Mississippi in the west to the Shenandoah and the edge of the coastal exclusion zone in the east. A respectable chunk of territory, most of it federated, and those settlements which hadn't federated—mostly in the east, where the anarchists lived at the edge of humanity— were at least not making any trouble. Their home down near Roan Mountain was as safe as safe could be, and was a part of something bigger, something so much greater. Part of a nation.

And the flames of Lauri's bottomless optimism were fanned to new heights, but Max brooded. This was as good a place as any to declare victory and turn their focus inward, but it seemed a job half-done; their enemies were still there, reuniting and rebuilding their power in their old strongholds in the prairies, but for all their success the FAA were at the end of their supply and the end of their rope and an end to the war could not have come at a better time. So Max brooded, because it didn't feel like victory, but more like kicking the can down the road for their grandbabies to deal with.

They both worked while Lauri dreamed and Max brooded, a picture of domestic bliss with Lauri bent over her writing desk while Max cleaned their rifles. They were both lifelong bookworms, though it was another way in which they were just alike yet so different; while Lauri agonized over philosophy and movement history and political economy, Max spent her time on names like Junger, von Klausewitz, Zhukov, Giap, and Xenophon, though she did find Trotsky's war diaries at least passable.

When she'd finished putting Lauri's battered old Winchester Model 70 back together, Max stood up, stretched, and walked over to her wife's desk. She'd always been big, even as a kid, and in middle age her scarred face and limping leg that war had left her with made her seem even bigger, dwarfing her petite and mousy little wife. The difference between them had always amused them both, and caused no end of amusement when those trouble-making women who'd eventually sided with the fascists anyways kept trying to guess which one of them had a dick.

And Max rested her hands on Lauri's shoulders and asked, "What are you working on, beautiful?"

Lauri didn't look up from her work, but she did lean back into the touch and sigh, "Y'know, I can almost believe it when you call me that."

"It's true. You're the prettiest girl in Kentucky and quite possibly the world."

"You're sweet."

"Whatcha working on, though?"

And Lauri did look up then, her sad brown eyes sparkling with excitement, and declared, "A constitution!"

"Really?"

"Well, a provisional one. I wanna have something to bring to the Army Council as soon as possible, before any arguing starts, so we can get on top of this whole nation-building thing the right way. Ashland down in Tennessee is where the most people live, so I'm gonna propose that for our new capitol, and I'm gonna suggest we call it the Ashland Confederated Republic, and--"

Max massaged her shoulders while she talked. She loved listening to Lauri talk; Lauri's voice was smooth as butter and sounded just like music, even if Max only understood about half of what she said.

"—and I'm excited, Max, I'm really excited. We're in the driver's seat of history right now! The Army Council could be a general assembly of workers' deputies, and this thing could be a workers' republic. Max, wouldn't that be wonderful?"

"Sure, sweetheart. But it's after midnight, and I know you're as fried as I am. You should come to bed. Your revolution will still be here in the morning."

"Not this time, Max. I need to finish this by morning so I can take it to the Army Council and get them talking about it before next midnight. It has to be today."

"What's so special about today?"

And Lauri laughed, and asked, "Max, do you know what

day tomorrow is? Or, it's midnight, so I guess what day today is."

"Uh . . . Saturday?"

"Max, it's the 30th. It's the 30th of April!"

That was a date that Bernardo had burned into all of their memories growing up, and that the FAA's political officers had burned into everybody else's over the past few years. April 30th, 1945 was the day that the red flag went up over a burning Berlin.

"Aw, shit," Max said, "it sure is. It's Victory Day."

"I want us to declare a Republic on Victory Day, Max. Just think about what kind of a story that would be! That's one of the most important things in the whole world, you know, is stories. Our grandbabies will talk about how we raised the red flag over the irradiated husk of Old America, 246 years after it went up over Germany, except for this time we'll finish the job."

"Did we finish the job, gorgeous? The bastards aren't really beat unless we can go north and capture Columbus, and we can't do that now and I don't know when we ever will."

"I know, Max. I know we had to make some hard choices about where to end the war, and I know we're leaving our grandbabies a pretty big mess to clean up. But we're gonna leave them an inheritance, too, and dammit it's gonna be a good one. We weren't just fighting for our lives these past few years, we were fighting for something historical, and we were fighting for our grandbabies, and y'know what? I think we did okay. Our kids and their kids aren't gonna go to bed hungry anymore, and when they tell stories about what we did here, I think they'll be pretty good stories."

"I hope so. We've worked our asses off, and I might know iron and lead better than I know economics, but I really do think what we've built here is gonna last. And I like the sound of that; I like the idea of being part of a story."

"We're all stories, Max. And the stories keep us going and keep us hopeful while we're here, and when we're gone our babies will tell stories about us. All this philosophy and political theory and all your military history, even, that's all it really is, is a bunch of stories; and, really, what could be more important than that?"

And Max buried her face in her wife's long, silky black hair and said, "God, babe, you're so smart."

"I know! It's pretty much the only thing I have going for me."

"That and these good looks. But I do want one thing from you."

"Oh?"

"Please come the fuck to bed. It's after midnight."

**[AD 2190, 125 years post-War;
somewhere in eastern Kentucky]**

MACK HAD BEEN AT WAR FOR MOST OF HER LIFE, BUT SHE
didn't think she'd ever get used to how heavy a sack full of
bombs actually was.

A thermite charge with enough oomph to disable a tank
could get downright beefy, and the quartermaster knew the
trick for packing six or seven into a duffel bag, which added
up to more weight than Mack liked to think about, especially
hauling it up and over the Kentucky hills, especially up to an
enemy position, especially in the middle of the damn night.
The United Christian Army were not known for their operational excellence, and it wasn't too much of a chore for four
partisans—well, three partisans and a girl scout—to get up

close and do the job, but the air in no man's land still smelled like death, the ground around them was pockmarked with shell craters, and if Mack squinted hard enough she could just make out the silhouettes of UCA sentries in the moonlight, and she reflected that it was always best to be careful. And unlike most Free Appalachian Army operators, Nakam Partisans wouldn't be taken prisoner if things broke bad. They'd be fortunate to just be shot on sight.

Which was, of course, why Mack had volunteered for the job.

The UCA brigade that had been giving them so much grief was dug into a lunette earthwork at a bend in the Ohio River, dug in too deep to dislodge, at least for the time being; the FAA fighters had gotten quite good at knocking out Father Covington's forts, but at this particular bend in the river they found themselves staring down the barrel of two thirds of the UCA's heavy armor. This particular hang-up wasn't much of a job for infantry, and the Free Appalachian Army was mostly infantry; but three Jews and four sacks of thermite could at least put a dent in it.

Getting over the wall was easy enough, as there were only four of them and the boneheads had quite a bit of earthwork to watch, and around 0200—right on schedule—they laid their saps right under the skirts of a few of the tanks behind the embankment just before the watchmen came back around and made a swift, clean egress. The timers on the saps gave them about half an hour to get far, far away, plenty of time, though Mack couldn't help being a bit disappointed; watching a thermite charge eat through tank tracks in the middle of the night would've been a beautiful sight to see.

Around 0245, fifteen minutes after the fascists woke up to their nasty surprise, the group reached their rendezvous point back over the lines and, after the obligatory round of high fives, Mack said, "Alright, who's got our bad-guy radio?"

"Right here, captain," one of the partisans replied, handing her a handheld two-way.

The political commissar, a funny little man in FAA combat fatigues, cocked an eyebrow and said, "Wait, hold up. Mack, why do you have a UCA radio? What are you planning?"

"We got it off that war cleric we merc'd yesterday," Mack said with a smirk. "I'm gonna ring up our friends and see what they think."

"No the hell you're not."

"Yeah the hell I am. I want them to know who did this. I want them to know it was Nakam Partisans who fucked 'em."

"Mack, this is dumb cowboy shit, and it's an OPSEC violation. What are you thinking?"

"You gonna stop me, girl scout?"

"Well, *captain*, stopping you from doing cowboy shit is why I'm here."

"No the hell it ain't. You're here to be a shop steward, and we already voted on it. The only way you're gonna stop me is to shoot me, and we both know you ain't gonna do that."

"I fucking might, *captain*."

"You shoot me, and the FAA loses my partisans. You lose my partisans, the federation loses Lexington Kibbutz. No Lexington Kibbutz, and the FAA can't hold New Lawrence. So go ahead and do it, girl scout; I'm sure that'll go over *very well* with the boss ladies."

The other two partisans flanked her to the left and right, their Kalashnikovs at low ready.

"Fine. Fine, go ahead and play your stupid little games."

"Thank you, comrade political commissar. I believe I will."

She turned on the radio, held it up to her mouth, and, laughing, said, "All call signs, all call signs, commo check. Can anybody hear me? Over."

A reply came at once, crystal-clear in the still night air: "I read you loud and clear, buddy. Who the hell is this? Over."

"Call sign Hammer 3, over."

"I ain't never heard of you. What unit are you with, Hammer 3? Over."

"Listen close, bonehead: My name is Mackie goddamn Blackadder, captain of the Nakam Partisans, Free Appalachian Army. Did y'all like our little fireworks show a minute ago?"

There was a long, satisfying pause, then: "I'm gonna fucking skin you alive, you goddamn reptile."

"Well, now that ten of your tanks have got piles of slag where their wheels used to be, I think that'd be a real neat trick. How many tanks does the UCA have left now, anyways? Are your foundries still producing new ones? *Oy gevalt*, trying to replace ten tanks while you're in the middle of losing a war; I sure don't envy you guys."

"I fucking swear to God, you are going to beg me to kill you before I'm done with you."

"Oh, really? Well, my name's Mackie Blackadder, and I'm the tall one with the big red hair; you can't miss me. And you know where to find me; I dunno if y'all have noticed, but there's a great big FAA cordon about a mile south of your position. Have a safe night, bonehead."

As the other two partisans snickered and the commissar rolled his eyes, Mack turned off the radio, handed it to him, and said, "Well, y'all, I ain't tired; let's head over to the TOC and see if our aunties are still awake."

The army camp was a hodgepodge of soldiers wearing clashing uniforms and holding various weapons, units of the hundred-odd nations that had federated under the Army Council. Even so early in the morning, it was full of activity, with couriers running to and from the command tent, soldiers clustered around their cooking fires, commissars getting in arguments. The constant reek of smoke and diesel fumes and gun oil made Mack feel right at home, and she smiled as she headed for the command tent, the olive drab canvas bigtop in the center of camp with the radio antenna sticking out of it. One of the other partisans had retired for the night, but the third—Josh, a pimply teenager in the thick of his first campaign, and Mack's self-appointed bodyguard—stuck by her side as she headed for the door of the tent. It was flanked by two soldiers in Ashlander uniforms.

"What's your business?" one of them asked.

"Just got back from a job, wanted to see the commandant before I hit the rack. That good enough for you, Steve?"

"Yeah, Mack. They want me to ask everybody that; 'What's your business?', all official-like. I feel like a fuckin clown, but I guess it's right, with so many boneheads around."

"Good man. Are our fearless leaders still in there?"

"Max is. Miss Lauri went to bed about an hour ago."

"That'll do."

The interior of the command tent was ordered chaos, a mess of tables stacked high with maps and paperwork, radios chattering, people arguing. Commandant Reyez was easy to spot even among all the hullabaloo; she was a solid six feet tall, broad, built like a brick shithouse, with a drum-fed RPD slung across her back where most soldiers would have a rifle. As Mack walked up, she was engaged in a spirited conversation with a grim-faced man in a long black duster.

"That dog won't hut, Max," the anarchist grumbled.

The commandant pinched the bridge of her nose. "And why not?"

"Boys ain't gonna take orders from up top."

"Alright, *fine*. What's it gonna take, Firelake? What do I gotta do to get my goddamn wasteland rangers?"

"Nah, that's the whole thing. All you gotta do is nuthin. You'll get your wasteland rangers soon as you let 'em off the leash."

"*Fine*. Consider it done. You know FAA units elect their own officers, anyways. Just . . . just get the Black Brigade into the field, alright?"

"Can do, ma'am. Thankee."

The scavenger thrust his hands into his pockets, turned around, and sauntered out of the tent without another word. The commandant let out a long, deep sigh and lit a cigarette.

Mack took advantage of the lull to step into the scavenger's place, where she snapped a crisp salute and barked, "Comrade Commandant! Comrade Captain Blackadder reporting back from the field, *ma'am!*"

Maxine sighed again. "What do you want, Mack?"

"Just wanted to let you know the job went okay. The Catholics got a real nice scare and now they're short at least ten AFVs."

"Well, that's some good news, at least."

"One of your wife's snitches wanted to shoot me."

"Did you get shot?"

"Nah."

"Then what are you whining about?"

Mack laughed and clapped her on the shoulder. "So, how goes the war, fearless leader?"

"*Puta madre.* You going to bed anytime soon?"

"Nah."

"Let's take a walk, you and me. I need some air."

"Can the kid come? He doesn't like leaving me alone."

"Sure. What's your name, kid?"

Josh blinked a few times, looking up at Max as though he were staring into the face of God. "Uh . . . I'm Joshua Bronstein, comrade commandant."

"My name is Max. Kid, how old are you?"

"Uh . . . I'm 19, co—Max."

"God, there's too many fucking kids here. So are you and Mack family or something?"

Josh withered beneath the question, too starstruck to respond. Mack put an arm across his shoulders and said, "He's my little cousin. We try to look out for each other, y'know?"

"Mmhmm."

As they headed out into the darkness, Max sighed again and asked, "So that trick you did with their tanks: You think you could pull that off again?"

Mack lit a cigarette and handed the pack to Josh. "Doubt it. Tell you the truth, fearless leader, I'm goddamn surprised tonight went as good as it did. I was expecting to come within sight of their earthworks and see too many guards. We got damn lucky, is what we did."

"Hell. We're in a bad situation here, Mack. We're

winning the war, but I'm getting worried we might lose the peace."

"The fuck does that mean?"

"Well, every pair of hands out here carrying a gun is a pair of hands that ain't doing anything useful. I dunno the specifics or how it all adds up—Lauri was always the economist, not me—but everybody's noticed by now, every month the food gets a little shittier and the portions get a little smaller. Same with ammo, and boots, and replacement parts, and what the fuck ever else."

"Yeah. I didn't wanna say nuthin, but yeah."

"Mmhmm. We're throwing everything we have into this war, and we're dominating in the field, but it is everything we have; we need some breathing room to start consolidating our base areas, or the FAA won't be able to operate for more than another year, tops. And the fascists won't be able to field an army south of the Ohio River pretty soon, but there's a hell of a lot of land and people and resources north of it, and I dunno if we'll *ever* be able to do anything about all that. Lauri could explain it better than me, but that's about where we're at. We can win the war, sure, but we need to give ourselves some room to breathe or we ain't gonna win the peace."

"*Feh.* So we hurry up with securing the Ohio Valley."

"Well, Mack, that brings us to this bullshit situation I find myself in right now. There's an entire goddamn armored brigade pinned in by the river. They can't advance because they know we'll just fall back and destroy them in detail in the hills. *We* can't advance because all I have is light infantry; we might be the best infantry in the world, but you can't fucking send light infantry against tanks. We can't starve 'em out because we can't do dick-all north of the river. And maintaining the cordon is tying up three of my flying columns."

"Hmm. Well, do you wanna know what I think?"

"By all means, comrade."

"Fascism is basically all aesthetics, right?"

"That's what Lauri says. All I know about it is how to shoot 'em."

She grinned a toothy, lopsided grin. "Did I tell you why our commissar got upset with me?"

"Nah."

"Yesterday, my boy Josh here stole a radio off of a dead war cleric. And tonight, after we fucked up their vehicles, I gave 'em a little call to let 'em know it was Nakam Partisans what that did it."

Max laughed and clapped her on the shoulder. "You just love poking the bear, don't you?"

"I do! But, Max, what do bears typically do after they been poked?"

"I reckon if you poke the bear, the bear's gonna bite."

"Mmhmm. The fascists aren't gonna take an insult like that lying down; their entire situation depends on saving face. But a bear that's short ten tanks is gonna have a bit less bite in it."

"Mackie Blackadder, you're dumb as a brick and you're

about as crazy as a rat in a tin shithouse, but I think you might be onto something."

"That's exactly what my dad used to say. Give it another day, maybe two, and *something* about this bullshit stalemate is gonna shift, or my great-granddaughter's a Trotskyist."

The last real armored brigade of Father Murphy Covington's United Christian Army didn't waste any time in responding to the insult, but the response certainly wasn't what Mack had expected.

She and Josh sat together behind the parapet in front of the FAA position, drinking too much coffee and playing cards as the sun rose up out of the exclusion zone. The ground between the cordon and the fascists was even more depressing under the sober light of day than it had been in the middle of the night; the verdant montaigne woodland covering most of the Ohio Valley stopped here, as though some titan had scoured the earth's surface, leaving them staring at a wasteland of dead trees and shell craters. The fortifications were just close enough together for Mack to sneak a peek at the fascists on a clear day, which allowed her good opportunities for rifle practice, but the morning after the raid dawned dreary and grey, and so she engaged in the much more important work of teaching Josh how to play blackjack. It was not going particularly well.

Shaking her head and scooping up the last of Josh's cigarettes, she said, "Dammit, kid, you don't *double down* on a 20, you *stand* on a 20. Stand. 20 is literally the second-best hand you can get."

"Sorry."

"It's fine, kid. You'll get it." She tossed him a pack of her cigarettes. "Clean out the bank one time and I'll teach you how to deal; dealing's easier. And once you learn how to deal, I'll teach you how to count cards."

"Mack, ain't that cheating?"

"What? Of course not. It's just math. Being good at a game ain't cheating. You wanna take a break, though? It don't look like you're having much fun."

Josh sighed with relief and lit one of the cigarettes. "Thanks, cuz. Say, can I ask you something?"

"Always."

"You got any big plans for what you're gonna do when the war's over?"

"I dunno. Go back to the kibbutz, I guess. Somebody's gotta grow all this tobacco we're burning."

"Well, I been thinking."

"Uh-oh."

"Yeah. I think I might wanna try out wasteland scrapping."

"Aw, hell, they're gonna ruin you. They'll make an anarchist out of you."

He shrugged. "I never really had much of a head for politics. Being a scavver just sounds like fun. Plus . . . Well, Mack, there's a girl."

"You met a cute anarchist?"

"Yeah."

"Yeah, that'll do it. Go track down Jack Firelake and talk to him, I guess; he'd be your guy for that. He'll probably give you a lecture about consensus decision-making and ask you to swear fealty to Makhnovia or whatever, though."

Josh shrugged again and filled up another cup of coffee, and the cousins sat together in congenial silence for a while before one of the soldiers up on the parapet shouted, "Hey, Mack, get your ass up here!"

"I'm fuckin *busy*, man!"

"There's somebody coming!"

She and Josh looked back and forth at each other for a beat before grabbing their rifles and running up the embankment. Sure enough, a group of about ten men in black UCA uniforms were strolling calmly towards them across no man's land, under a white flag.

"Well, I'll be goddamned," Mack pontificated. "This has gotta be some kinda trick."

"What the hell did you guys do last night?"

"All we did was sabotage some AFVs, man. They'd have to be a lot worse off than we thought for some sabotaged vehicles to spark negotiations."

"So what do you think?"

"Uh . . . Me and Josh will hold 'em here, I guess. You go get the commandant. And the subcommandant."

"Alright. I'll be back in a minute."

They drew down on the approaching group, and Josh whispered, "Mack, what the hell do we do?"

"I'm trying to make my mind up. I don't wanna merc people under a white flag, but also I don't know if fascists count as people."

When they were about 30 meters out, Mack shouted, "Alright, that's close enough! You take one more step and we shoot!"

The group halted.

"State your business!"

The group of ten parted, and an eleventh stepped forward from their rear. Rather than combat fatigues, he wore the long black robes and collar of a war cleric. He was tall, taller than Mack, with a head of long, gorgeous blonde hair, crystal blue eyes, and a wide, jovial smile that seemed just a bit too enthusiastic. He cupped his hands around his mouth and called out, "Good morning! May we come into your camp? We are under a flag of truce, as you can see."

"That's for the commandant to decide, fancypants. Till she gets here, y'all stay right the fuck put. Now what do you want?"

"We wish only to talk, my good lady."

"And what about?"

The war cleric smirked. "I take it you must be the famous Mackie Blackadder. What a small world."

"Oh, we got Sherlock Holmes over here. What gave it away?"

"Are you always so discourteous to your guests?"

"Nah, just you in particular. Now what do you want?"

"I will await your commandant. We do not parley with the help."

"I'm gonna tell her you said that."

A moment later, an armed platoon came up out of the camp, led by two women: Maxine, and a small, mousy Cherokee woman wearing thick coke bottle glasses and a long gingham dress. Mack and Josh trailed along behind as the group went over the earthwork and surrounded the fascists, who looked more and more uncomfortable. To their surprise, it wasn't Max, but Lauri who stepped up to the war cleric and, staring down at her boots, said, "State your business."

Her voice was quiet, almost subdued, but it dripped with authority. The war cleric stood speechless for a moment, then gave an exaggerated bow and said, "Ah, you must be the legendary Laurelei Bluecrow. It is an honor to make the acquaintance of such a worthy opponent, sir."

All of the FAA soldiers gasped in unison. Max growled like a hungry dog and started to take a step forward; Lauri put out a hand to stop her, looked up into the war cleric's eyes, and asked, "Would you like to try that again?"

"I, ah . . . I meant no offense, my good lady."

"Yes, you did. Now, who are you?"

He bowed again. "I am Lazar Stojanovic Wenden, war cleric of the United Christian Army and Archdeacon of God's true church. I come under orders from our Patriarch himself."

"And to do what?"

"We bring terms of ceasefire, and I think you will be very amenable to them; they are quite reasonable."

Lauri looked up at Max, and the two women nodded in silent understanding. Lauri lowered her head and scurried back to the rear of the group. Max cracked her neck, held her RPD over her shoulder, and said, "I take it you know who I am."

"Oh, indeed. There is not a soldier in black who hasn't heard the name of Maxine Mondragon Reyez, niece of the late Bernardo. It is, again, an honor to stand face-to-face with such an opponent."

"Wish I could say the same; I ain't never heard of you before in my life, and I'd remember a name as crazy as yours. Hand over your weapons and we can talk."

"I trust they will be returned to us upon our departure?"

"Nope."

The envoys looked dubiously at the two dozen rifle barrels pointed at them and started unslinging their Armalites, drawing their Colts, and handing them over. Lazar pulled aside his vestments to draw his sidearm, revealing a three-foot arming sword hanging from his pistol belt. The

FAA fighters facing him gawked at him for a moment, and several burst into laughter. Mack shouldered her way to the front of the group, cackling, "Holy shit, check out Mad Jack Churchill over here!"

"I must respectfully refuse to surrender my sword," the war cleric said. "It is a priceless family heirloom."

"Alright, King Arthur," Max replied, rolling her eyes. "It ain't like you can do anything with it. Just . . . Man, why the hell are you carrying a *sword* into battle in the 22nd goddamn century?"

Lazar's eye twitched. "An officer who goes into battle without his sword is not properly dressed. I am a man of the cloth, but I hold a colonel's rank."

Mack slapped her thigh and wheezed, "My man straight-up brought a knife to a gunfight."

"My ancestor carried this sword against the Oriental hordes at Kosovo eight hundred years ago, and every scion of our family has carried it since, as befits a military man of rank and lineage."

The FAA fighters laughed harder. The uniformed fascists around him surveyed the rifles still trained on them and looked decidedly uncomfortable. Mack doubled over cackling like a witch. When she stood up straight, Lazar fixed her with a withering look; there was murder in his eyes, but his smile grew wider, and he hissed, "If I remember correctly, such weapons were put to good use at Treblinka."

He'd expected the barb to rattle her, but instead she

pumped her fist in front of her crotch and hooted, "Oh, good one, man. I am *so* triggered, I am so-ass triggered. Yeah, I'm sure these negotiations are gonna go *great*."

With a sigh, Max pushed her back and grumbled, "Mackie, quit playing with your food. Listen, Lazarus--"

"Lazar."

"Whatever. We've got enough of the Army Council here to form a quorum, so yeah, come with us and we can sit down and formally accept your unconditional surrender. Somebody go find Jack Firelake and Catahecassa and tell 'em to get their asses over here and we'll get hot chow dished out. What do fascists eat for breakfast?"

"You people call everyone you don't like a fascist," Lazar said, rolling his eyes. "We are *traditionalist populists*. Fascism is a godless ideology."

"Didn't stop you from federating with Rockwell's Volunteers. And it sure felt fashy when y'all burned out our towns. Now shut the fuck up."

Lazar shut the fuck up. Mack fell back into the rear of the group as they headed into the camp, and Josh grabbed her shoulder and whispered, "I have got a really bad feeling about this."

"Well, you're a smart kid."

"What was it that he said to you? I know I've heard that name before."

"Treblinka. It was one of the camps in the Shoah. The guy in charge of the showers used to wave around a sword and cut bits off of people if they weren't queueing up to die fast enough."

"Well, I'm gonna fucking kill him, then."

"Oh, me too. But I bet you a carton of smokes that the boss ladies are gonna beat us to it."

They cleared off the biggest table in the command tent and sat the delegation across one side of it, flanked by a team of scavengers from the anarchist settlements, hard-faced wasteland rangers in black leather dusters. As the Army Council delegates took seats across from them, Lazar took a look around and said, "I must say, this is all highly irregular."

"How's that?" Maxine asked, taking a seat and lighting a smoke.

"You must admit it is highly irregular for peace negotiations to take place under arms."

"If you don't wanna talk to us, you can leave."

Lazar chewed his bottom lip and said nothing. Mack took a seat next to Max, with Josh standing behind her, his Kalashnikov at low ready, and Lazar glared daggers at her and hissed, "Why is *it* here?"

"I'm on the Army Council," Mack said, grinning. "I'm a regional delegate for a third of the farms in New Lawrence and I'm the captain of their partisans. Oh, did you not know that?"

"It is to be expected, I suppose. The march of the rootless cosmopolitan echoes ever down through the ages."

"You sure do talk a lot of shit for a guy with no guns."

"We are under a flag of truce!"

"Hey, you ever read Thucydides?"

"What? Of course I've read Thucydides; I am an educated gentleman. What's that got to do with anything?"

"Oh, chief, that's got everything to do with anything. *The strong do what they will, and the weak suffer what they must.*"

"So you fancy yourself the strong, then?"

"You were the ones who came to us, Lazarus."

"My name is *Lazar!* It's Serbian."

"At this rate my strap is gonna *Ser-be-in* your dad before we get any work done."

Maxine rested a hand on her shoulder and grumbled, "Mackie, quit playing with your food. Alright, Archdeacon, what bill of goods are you trying to sell us?"

Lazar's smile returned. "Thank you, commandant. As I said before, I bring terms for a temporary cessation of hostilities, and I carry the mandate of Father Covington himself. This stalemate we've found ourselves in profits nothing for both sides, and we are all eager to move on with our lives. So, in exchange for an indemnity and some territorial concessions —which are, I think, quite reasonable—our brigade will hand you this salient and withdraw over the river. I hope we can quickly work out the particulars of the indemnity and concessions; I'm due for a few weeks of leave time, and my children miss their papa."

The Army Council looked back and forth at one another for a beat, then, in unison, burst into mocking laughter. Lazar blushed and his smile hardened, and Mack slapped the table and cackled, "Oh, the *balls* on this one! The big, fat cast-iron *balls* on this one!"

"Is there a problem?"

Laurelei Bluecrow composed herself, studied the table in front of her, and muttered, "The Army Council unilaterally rejects your terms."

"Whyever for?"

"Let me make you a counter-offer," Maxine said, poking the air with the end of her cigarette. "Your brigade will hand over all weapons, vehicles, ordnance, and other war material, along with your regimental colours, and we'll allow you to go back over the river unharmed."

"And what on Earth would you give us in return?"

"I just said: Your lives. Out of the goodness of my heart, I'll magnanimously allow you assholes to go back to Ohio. Don't that sound nice?"

She read the faces of the other fascist delegates and determined that, yes, that did sound very nice to everyone but Lazar. As he stewed in growing indignation, one of them turned to him and whispered, "Boss, I think that's the best we're gonna get."

"You say this as if you're offering terms to a defeated opponent," the archdeacon grumbled.

"Well," Max said, "y'all kinda are."

"The United Christian Army has never been defeated in the field!"

"Really? That's new information. Last time I checked, we've spent the past two years whipping y'all all up and down the Ohio Valley. When you're trying to offer terms, you ought to be doing it from a position of strength; and to tell you the truth, kid, I'm more than half tempted to just give you whatever territorial concessions you'll ask for, on account of I know you'll never be able to hold them."

"You know you'll never be able to dislodge our garrison, commandant."

"Don't need to. Here's how it is, kid: You accept my terms, or I break the cordon and leave."

"You're . . . threatening . . . to withdraw? You're 'threatening' to quit the field?"

"Our being here is the only reason you're here," Lauri said, accepting a cigarette from Max. "If the FAA pulls out of the area, you no longer have a reason to stay bivouacked in a secure fixed position. You could advance and break our cordon at any time, but you won't, because you know that we'll just destroy your force in detail in the hills. So, yes, we are threatening to withdraw and to remove your excuse for staying safe. I think that your commanding officers will probably not be as sensitive to the tactical fix you're in as we are."

"So that's what's on the table here," Max said. "You can either withdraw peacefully today or withdraw under fire next week. Or you can stay put and eat a court martial for cowardice. What happens at fascist courts martial, anyways? Are they understanding of the realities of partisan warfare?"

Though his smile didn't waver, Lazar ground his teeth and said nothing.

"Those are your choices, kid. You can walk away from it and live another day, die from an FAA sharpshooter's bullet in a week or two, or die a coward's death at the end of a rope back in Columbus. Up to you."

"Are you attempting to call me a coward?"

"Nah. But your superiors will if you don't die for them fast enough. Are you in a big hurry to die, kid? You mentioned you've got little ones; do you want them to grow up without their papa?"

"Your terms are unacceptable."

"This the reality of the military situation," Lauri said. "We are the ones negotiating from a position of strength, and the best thing you can do right now is to recognize realities."

"And what would *you* know about recognizing realities?"

Lauri rolled her eyes. Max snarled like a dog and looked like she was about to leap over the table and tear Lazar Wenden's throat out. But, before anyone else could move, one of the other fascists stood up and started to walk away.

One of the wasteland rangers shoved a rifle barrel into his

face and said, "Alright, buddy, what's the big idea? Where are we going?"

The fascist met his eyes and said, in a calm and even tone, "I surrender."

"Huh?"

"I've spent the past two years getting dick-whipped up and down the Appalachian Mountains, I've spent the past six weeks bivouacked on the bank of a river staring at home, and my war cleric is determined to turn down our only shot at getting out of this mess alive. My name is Jacob Stockdale, I'm a major in the United Christian Army, and I surrender."

Lazar's smile didn't waver, but his eyes twitched, and he ground his teeth so hard it seemed they were about to shatter. On the other end of the table, three more men stood up and walked over to the wasteland rangers. Mack clapped her hands and hooted, "Aw hell, looks like I was wrong. These negotiations are going pretty damn good after all."

"Cowards!" the archdeacon shouted. "You four are nothing but treasonous cowards! And may you find a coward's grave!"

"They have sense, Lazar," Laurelei said calmly. "This theater of the war is practically wrapped up already, no matter what happens here today. You should listen to your men and accept a path to peace. With apologies to my Maxine, I'll tell you the truth: If you go over the river, we won't be able to follow you. Just go."

The archdeacon sprung up from his chair, his smile

finally cracking into a look of murderous rage, and he hissed, "I am not . . . I am *not* going to listen to this sort of talk from a *mud-skinned Bolshevist faggot!*"

Lauri rolled her eyes again. Max gripped the table as though it were about to splinter in her hands. And Mackie Blackadder laughed harder and cackled, "*Oh shit*, there it is! Listen, chief, you got us all fucked if you think you're ever gonna walk out of here alive after calling Miss Lauri the faggot word."

"And I'll certainly not listen to it from *you*, merchant."

"That's why you assholes are losing the war, y'know. You're all so full of piss and vinegar that there ain't no room left over for brains. Honestly, I wanna know who the hell was the brain genius who sent *you* to negotiate a ceasefire."

"I, unlike you godless, conniving Bolshevists, am a man of honor! I came here offering generous, magnanimous terms, and you lot have been so . . . disrespectful! Difficult!"

On the far end of the table, Jack Firelake kicked his feet up and folded his hands behind his head. "Mmhmm," he pontificated. "You brought terms, and they was rejected. We ain't had a vote on it or nuthin, but it sounds like consensus to me. That's politics, kid."

"I'll not stand for this! I am leaving, and then I am going to come back here with my brigade behind me and hang these traitors and kill all of you . . . you *subhumans*."

"Like you been doin for the past two years?"

Maxine Reyez stood up, cracked her back, and said, "Actually, I don't think you are."

"Oh, so *now* you're open to negotiations, you godless Bolshevist mud?"

"Ol' Mackie Blackadder over there has got quite the mouth on her, but the worst thing about that is that she always tells the truth. And she's right. Nobody fucking talks to my wife like that."

Her tone was calm, almost emotionless, as though she were making idle conversation, but the whole of the Army Council gasped in unison. While the others chewed their bottom lips and studied the table, Lauri got up, grabbed Max's arm, and said, "Sweetie, you don't . . . you don't need to do this."

"I do, babydoll. I really do."

"And just what do you intend to do, woman?" Lazar sneered. "Are you going to criticize me? Shall we have a struggle session?"

"Somethin like that. Here's another counteroffer for you, fancypants: You and me, outside. And negotiations are over, so this is *just* about you and me; if you win, you and the six flunkies you've got left can walk away. And when I win, those guys can do whatever they want. You been talking big all day, kid, but now it's time to throw hands."

"Are you . . . challenging me to a duel?"

"I figured Sir Chivalry over here would be all horny for that. Call it whatever you want; I'm just really, really in a mood to beat your ass. Or you can run away, like the prissy yellow coward we all know you are."

"I am a Wenden, commandant, and a Wenden does not run. How shall we conduct this challenge?"

"Oh, I've got some notions about that. Laurelei, beautiful, do me a favor: We've got that trunk with all Bernardo's old shit in it here with us, right?"

Lauri Bluecrow smiled as she examined her boots and said, "Yeah, Max. Yeah, we sure do."

Lazar wasn't sure what to expect next, because none of the FAA soldiers would speak to or acknowledge him after they left the command tent. Maxine Reyez led him to an open patch of ground beneath the earthwork and left him there, walking off to stand with her assembled troops. So the archdeacon drew his sword, thrust it into the ground, knelt before it, and prayed.

Though the unknown quantity of Reyez' cryptic instructions played on his nerves, he felt no fear. Whatever was about to happen, he was sure it would be no contest. He felt sure of his own abilities, and this would be far from his first kill; and, more importantly, he was a white man, while she was a subhuman Bolshevist homosexual. Even in a fallen world, in an age of degeneracy, over a hundred years since nuclear fire rained from the skies and Old

America burned, being a white man still counted for something.

As he prayed, he glanced over to the other side of the field and noticed that, of the ten delegates who'd come across the lines with him, three now remained. Just as well; it was fitting that he should make his stand alone. Soon, the cowards would get a demonstration of what a brave man can do.

After a few minutes, Lauri Bluecrow came running through the camp, holding a long, thin bundle of rags over her shoulder, filling the air with the smell of cloves and cosmoline. She slid to a stop beside Max, and Max took the bundle from her and began to unwrap it, drawing forth a beautiful, swept-hilt Spanish rapier, four feet long from tang to tip. She held it up and did a quick moulinet, testing its weight, and the oversized weapon looked like a toy in her massive hand. Lauri grabbed her arm, stretched up to plant a kiss on her lips, and said, "Promise me you'll be careful, Max. Please be careful. You're always getting yourself hurt."

"I'll be careful, beautiful. This shouldn't take too long."

"And . . . this is childish, and it's probably reactionary, but can I say something?"

"Of course."

"I don't think I've ever been more turned on than I am right now."

"Ha! Y'know, I figured."

"A giant butch with a sword is about to go defend my honor. What's a girl to think?"

Max pulled her in close and kissed her. "Maybe after I dispatch this asshole, I'll crown you the queen of love and beauty."

"Oh, I would die. But I'm serious, Max; *please* be careful."

"I will, babydoll. I always am."

"No, you're not. I love you, Max."

"I love you, too, Lauri. This won't take long."

Max walked a few paces toward the kneeling Lazar and growled, "Alright, kid, let's get this over with."

The archdeacon smirked as he got to his feet. "So it's to be steel against steel, then? I like that very well. And that is a beautiful sword."

"It was Bernardo's; he was a sentimental bastard. I was gonna just beat you to death with a rifle butt, like how an adult might merc somebody, but I figured you'd prolly get off on dying on the end of Bernardo Reyez's parade piece."

"Spoken barbarically and uncouthly, as fits a person of your station, but I will admit, it is poetic. I look forward to cleaning your blood off of my steel tonight; I only hope that the mud won't leave a stain."

"God, you're irritating."

As soon as the words left her mouth, Max moved, closing the gap between them in a few quick strides. She moved rigidly, more like a fencer than a killer, but it caught Lazar by surprise—he'd been readying a verbal retort, unaware that combat had started—and he only just managed to dodge a high lunge that skewered the air where his throat had been a moment before. He recovered with a cry of shock and rage, throwing a strike at Max's midsection; she caught it on her blade and reposted, tearing a wide, ugly rent in his vestments. The FAA fighters cheered.

They traded blows back and forth like a whirlwind for a heated few seconds, and Lazar noted that his first impression —more like a fencer than a killer—had been correct; Max's style was inflexible, rehearsed, predictable. She'd underestimated him, and this wasn't her kind of fight. He parried another of her lunges, saw an opening, and reposted, slashing at her face. The stroke made contact, biting into her cheek and spraying blood across the grass, prompting gasps of shock and outrage from the onlookers and a roar of bestial rage from Max. She didn't pause, but counterattacked, and the fury of it forced him backward and nearly threw him off his footing; he felt his left hand grow wet and slick and realized that he'd been wounded as well, though in the speed of the onslaught he couldn't tell when.

Just as Lazar began to think he'd miscalculated, Max reared her sword-arm back and swung the rapier like a cleaver, putting all of her strength into a haymaker blow that would end the fight if it landed. He lunged into her guard and laughed aloud as he blocked the stroke and followed up, crossing their blades and flicking the rapier out of her hand. It flew through the air and stuck quivering in the grass a few yards away.

He took a step back and, laughing, declared, "See? You're nothing! Swordcraft is a man's work. You were never going to-_"

In that split second, Max closed the distance between them and swung her fist into his face. He staggered backward, spitting blood and teeth, and she followed up with a kick to his stomach, dropping him to his knees. She grabbed a fistful of his long, blonde hair and held his head up as she drove her fist into it again, and again, and again. The wet, packing sound of the blows was drowned out by the cheering crowd; loudest of all was Mackie Blackadder, who jumped up and down and hooted, "Oh, yeah! You get his ass, commandant! You *get! His! Ass!*"

Max released the archdeacon's hair and he crumpled into a heap on the ground. She picked up his arming sword from where it had fallen beside him, put the tip under his chin, spit out a mouthful of blood, and slurred, "We done here?"

Lazar's eyes lost focus for a moment. He drew in a weak, ragged breath, coughed up a lungful of blood, and wheezed, "P . . . please . . ."

"Speak up. I'm a little hard of hearing."

"P . . . please . . . My . . . my children . . ."

"Are you asking for quarter?"

He coughed again, struggling to breathe. "It . . . it *hurts* . . ."

"Wow. You have never gotten your ass beat before, have you?"

"Mercy . . . My children . . . Mercy . . ."

"Your kids are probably just as fucked up as you are."

The archdeacon gagged, spat up a molar, and wheezed, almost too weakly to hear: "P . . . please . . ."

Speaking was becoming difficult, but Max spat out another mouthful of blood and slurred, "Spoken like a real American."

And, pointing the sword at the two remaining UCA delegates: "You two, get over here and pick up your trash."

Lauri was the first to reach them. She threw her arms around Max, put a tentative hand on her flayed cheek, and said, "Oh. Oh, that's going to need stitches."

"Gonna leave a good scar, at least. Hey, Mack!"

Mack came running over. "What's up, boss lady?"

"You want a free sword?"

"Oh, I would fucking love a free sword."

Lazar had managed to roll himself over and prop himself up on his elbows as he coughed up more blood. He glanced up to watch the commandant hand Mack the Wenden family sword, then groaned and collapsed back onto the grass. The two other fascists walked up, not too quickly, and pulled Lazar to his feet, holding him up between them as his head lolled to one side and he groaned with pain, shame, and impotent rage. One of them looked over to Max and Lauri and asked, "Do the terms of withdrawal still stand?"

"Sure," Max slurred. "Surrender your arms, equipment, and regimental colours, and we'll let y'all leave. Sorry-not-sorry I broke your friend, but to be fair I think his stupid face broke my fuckin hand."

"He's not our friend. And if he survives this, I think he's gonna have a long, rough recovery."

At the foot of the earthwork, Mackie and Josh sat down across from each other, pulling out a deck of cards and a few packs of cigarettes, the day's excitement already forgotten in favor of more important business. As Mack shuffled and started to deal, Josh asked, "So what are you gonna do with the sword?"

"I dunno," Mack said. "Probably give it to some girl. Girls love swords, y'know."

"Can I have it?"

"What? Sure, I guess. I don't really need it for nuthin. What do you want it for?"

"Gonna give it to a girl."

"Oh, *mazel tov*. And that's a good idea, too; girls love swords."

I.

**[AD 2265, 200 years post-War;
Coal Mountain, Georgia]**

Ferrel was giving a lecture about the history of development projects in the Chattahoochee Valley. Sean and Iris were not paying attention.

Not that Ferrel was an easy man to ignore. He was tall, about six feet, scarred and haggard from a lifetime of hard work. He was an anarchist, and looked the part in his flannel work shirt and long black duster with a pair of fiery red eyes glaring out of a wild shock of unkempt hair and a long, wiry beard. And Ferrel didn't speak, but *growled*, in a voice laced with cigarette smoke and cordite. But Iris and Sean were both sixteen and had more important things on their minds.

In the back of the Greater Atlanta Ecological Research Institute's infoshop, not quite out of sight of the others, Sean looked deep into her eyes and stroked her cheek and whispered, "You're so pretty."

Iris winced as his fingers brushed the stubble under her chin—the base was inside the Atlanta Exclusion Zone, a few days' travel from any permanent settlements, without many amenities, and shaving with a straight razor was an art she was still getting the hang of—but his touch lingered on the spot, and he gave her a quick scritch, like a cat, and pecked her on the lips. She smiled and whispered back, "You're so sweet, Sean."

"You're so fucking pretty, babe."

Sean looked like a miniature version of his father, wearing the wasteland ranger's ubiquitous long black duster, his wavy brown hair pulled back into a ponytail, the patchy beginnings of a beard sprouting across his round, young face. Iris wore a flannel work shirt and a pair of overalls, like an Ashlander state ecologist in miniature, along with a denim patch vest, and she kept her hair shaved on the sides and styled into a perfect DA. She held Sean's hands in both of hers and whispered, "I'm so glad you're here, Sean."

He extracted one of his hands, rested it on her thigh, and stammered, "Hey, I . . . I . . ."

"You can say it, sweetie."

"I love you."

They kissed, and from the front of the room Ferrel barked, "Oi! Pay attention!"

They looked forward without breaking their embrace, and Sean gave a sheepish smile and said, "Yeah. Sorry, Pops."

Ferrel rolled his eyes. "We're heading out for Shady Grove in *two days*, people. Now, *as I was saying*, scavengers that have gone that way report that the Lanier reservoir is still filled, meaning Buford Dam is still standing. However, it ain't been operational in all this time, meaning the lake has been accumulating sediment for the past two hundred years, so the whole character of it has changed from anything the pre-War records might have to say. Most scavver expeditions have been focused on cracking open Old DC, so the Atlanta Exclusion Zone is still unexplored territory for the most part. The reservoir could be a big green spring in the middle of the wasteland, or it could be a radiation sink full of toxic mud. Only one way to find out. The expedition is to be a rough initial survey of the area. We'll go check out the lake at Shady Grove, and if it looks safe, we'll probe some of the outlying islands and try to map a route to a couple of industrial facilities and the Old American National Guard station on the other side."

That got the kids' attention. Iris stared ahead with a faraway look in her eyes and muttered, "Islands. If the lake is safe, those islands could host pre-War vegetation without much contamination. And if it's not safe, hell, I still wanna see the mutations. Ionizing radiation does wild shit to conifers."

And Sean looked ahead with his own obsessions dancing in his mind, and he whispered, "Nobody from up north has done an Atlanta run like this before. It could all be untouched. God, that would be a lot of scrap."

As the meeting adjourned and the group got up and went their separate ways, with decks of cards and jugs of wine appearing out of rucksacks, the two kids got up and disappeared into the darkness. Ferrel sat down against the wall and lit a cigarette, and he waved as he saw Lilly, the facility director, walking up to him. She was a tall, Black woman with a warm face, wearing a long gingham dress embroidered with a state ecologist's badge on the left shoulder. She grinned as she approached and asked, "Pretty exciting, huh?"

"Mmhmm. I ain't gonna lie, though; I'm a bit worried about the boy."

"Ah, if he's half the scavver you are, he'll be fine."

"Listen, Lilly, are you . . . are you sure it's a good idea to bring both of 'em along?"

"Heh. I figured that's what you were talking about. You said Sean wants in on the family business, right?"

"Oh, yeah. He loves this shit. Hell, he might be a bigger waster than I am."

"Well, Iris is one of the best ecologists I've got, young as she is. And even if we brought just one of 'em, do you really think the other one would stay behind?"

"Nah, see, that's just what I'm worried about. Them two are gonna be . . . distracted."

"They're smart kids, Ferrel. I'm worried about a lot of things, but I ain't worried about the kids. They know what they're doing about as much as we do."

"It ain't that I doubt their competence. I just know they're young and in love and rebellious and horny. What is it you reckon they're doin right now?"

Lilly shrugged. "Fucking, probably."

"Yeah. We're gonna be out in the middle of God-knows-what and I worry there ain't gonna be enough blood left over to run their brains with."

"You worry too much, Ferrel. Even if they do turn stupid —and yeah, they probably will—we've got a good team here. The objective is only a few days away."

"Ah, reckon you're right."

"I'm always right."

He laughed. "Still, I dunno how I feel about my boy fallin for one of you tankies. No offense."

"We're not tankies, Ferrel, we're Trotskyists."

"Ah, you're all authoritarians to me."

Lilly rolled her eyes. "Yeah, Ferrel. I know."

The facility had been a high school before the War, and the folks coming down from the mountains up north had wasted no time in converting it, with the few serviceable buildings turned into barracks and laboratories and the wide open spaces filled up with tents and greenhouses and model gardens where crops and produce and native flora grew nestled around the trees. The place was far enough south from the Ashlander cities and far enough north from the settlements in the swamps to be free from any light pollution, and at night the staff could see a sky studded with big, bright stars, casting enough silver light to spot the detachments of Ashlander soldiers and Freesider wasteland rangers patrolling the perimeter and to pick out the individual loblolly pines growing out of what had once been a football field.

Sean and Iris had climbed up onto the roof of the forestry laboratory, the building where Iris worked most days, to watch the stars, though Iris had right away fixed her attention on the football field and, at Sean's prompting, launched into a lecture about the plants being propagated there, their rate and character of growth, and the soil toxicity levels. She was rattling off a list of trivia about loblolly pine trees when Sean muttered, "Wow, babe, you're so fuckin smart."

She blushed and examined her lap. He kissed her cheek and she blushed harder, scooted a few inches away from him, and, panting, fished a pack of cigarettes out of her pocket and lit one.

"Y'know those are bad for you," Sean said.

"Yeah, but they help me think."

"You smell like an ashtray."

"Oh. Sorry." She looked away.

"No, no, I didn't mean it like that. *Shit.* I meant . . . I like that I can recognize all these things about you. Iris smells like cigarettes and pine tar and roses."

She smiled and scooted closer to him. "And Sean smells like gun oil and sweat and leather. I . . . I really like that I know that. I like that we've been able to spend so much time together."

"Me, too. You excited about the trip?"

"Oh, yeah. This is gonna be great. The Atlanta Exclusion Zone has been mostly untouched from the north since the War, and the environmental changes are like totally undocumented. I can't wait to see it. It's gonna be fascinating."

"You're so smart, babe."

"Aw, jeez. Thanks."

He rested a hand on her thigh, and she leaned into the embrace. The hand wandered between her legs. She tensed up, stifled a yelp, almost dropped her cigarette. Sean pulled the hand away and stammered, "Oh, shit, was that . . . was that bad?"

"Well, no, but . . . I've been worried, Sean. Worried you'd, y'know . . . mind."

"Mind what?"

"Well, Sean, you . . . you *know*. I'm . . . different."

He cocked an eyebrow. "Different how?"

"I have a dick, Sean."

"Well yeah, you told me that already. So do a lot of girls."

She laughed and leaned against him. "You're so fucking stupid, Sean, but you're sweet."

"Yeah, well, what does that make you?"

"A moronsexual."

He held her tight, exploring her with his hands, but after a few minutes he stopped, tensed up, drew in a deep breath.

"What's up?" she asked.

"Uh . . . it's nothing."

"You nervous?"

"Uh . . . yeah. Yeah, Iris, I'm nervous."

"Don't be. I like you a lot, Sean."

"I . . . I really like you, too, Iris."

She turned and looked into his eyes then, and said, in a matter-of-fact way: "We should have sex."

"I . . . I'd like that. I'd like that a lot. But I don't . . . ah . . ."

"You new at this?"

"Well, I've been with a girl before, but . . ."

"Not a girl like me?"

"Yeah."

She smirked. "Don't worry, dummy. I'll show you."

The team was made up of six field researchers—including Lilly and Iris—four Ashlander soldiers in their flecktarn uniforms, and four Freesider wasteland rangers in their black dusters, including Sean and Ferrel. The Ashlanders, soldiers and scientists, carried Kalashnikov battle rifles over their shoulders, while the Freesiders each carried a different weapon suited to their individual taste; Sean had an ancient Winchester Model 70 across his back, archaic but accurate. And each of them bore a rucksack bristling with gear and supplies, with the ecologists more heavily laden than the others. Iris carried a messenger bag over her left shoulder and had a double-bit felling axe dangling from the side of her rucksack. She was small compared to the others, and the overabundance of kit made her look rather like a turtle.

As they milled about inside the perimeter fence and waited for the sun to rise, one of the scavengers and one of the soldiers had gotten into a spirited argument, a favorite pastime whenever the two groups were together; the scavvers, Freesiders, were all anarchists, and the Ashlanders had brought along a political officer. The argument ended without concluding as both participants ran out of words and walked off rolling their eyes. As the scavver, a tall woman with black hair shaved on one side and a trail carbine over her shoulder, headed back toward her companions at the front of the group, she stopped by Iris and Sean, looked down at Iris, and said, "Oh, hey there, baby butch. I was hoping they'd drag you along."

"Hey," Iris said with a half-hearted wave.

"I've seen you around camp but never had a chance to say anything. I fucking love your hair, kid."

"Thanks."

"What do you style it with out here?"

"Beeswax."

"Right on. Listen, if you need anything, you can come find me, alright? My name's Cathy."

"I'm Iris."

"Right on. Girls like us gotta stick together, right?"

Cathy gave Sean's shoulder a squeeze as she continued on to the front of the group, where Ferrel stood surveying the sky with his sharp, tired eyes. The sky was gunmetal grey, with black thunderheads gathering in the northeast, and the air smelled of ozone and repressed potential. The pines and sycamores quaked in the growing north wind, and Ferrel glared up at it all and grumbled, "Mmhmm."

Sean pushed his way to the front of the group and stood at Ferrel's side, imitating his movements and mannerisms. Lilly walked up to both of them and asked, "Well, ranger, how bad do you think it's gonna be?"

"Could be a rough one," he grumbled. "I don't like the look of them anvils in the sky up there."

"Shoot. I sure hope it blows itself out before we hit the lake. Gonna be miserable to walk through, too."

"What's the matter? Are reds scared to get wet?"

The wasters all laughed. Lilly and the four soldiers rolled their eyes.

"Sun's up now. We ought to go ahead and get rolling, eat up some miles before it hits. Alright, folks; weapons loose, and let's get walking."

The group swung their rifles around to low ready and moved forward at an easy pace, the scavvers leading the way, soldiers bringing up the rear, ecologists in the middle. Iris trotted a bit faster and fell into place beside Sean, just behind Ferrel in the order. She walked with ease, seeming not to notice the weight of all her kit and equipment, and Sean and the other scavvers looked on her with approval. Ferrel offered her just a hint of a smile and gave her shoulder a squeeze.

The land so far south was mostly flat, and the road into town, though fallen to pieces with age, still presented a recognizable and mostly clear path; the roads north and west were choked with the ancient wrecks of automobiles rusting away in an eternal gridlock, but the rest was clear save for a bit of prairie grass and undergrowth and the occasional sapling. Typical for an exclusion zone, the foliage just south of the facility grew differently than it did up in the mountains, with lush and verdant undergrowth and strong young trees growing up in the shadows of dead, ancient trees unnaturally preserved. While the others kept their eyes on the road ahead and on the decaying buildings that loomed like tombstones out of the verge on either side of it, Iris took mental notes on the state of the trees. The older trees, and especially the dead ones, were not healthy; they grew up too quickly, with sickening knobs and half-formed branches studding the lower trunks like keloid scars and tight crowns of thick, shaggy branches at the top, typical mutations for trees exposed to ionizing radiation. Their daughters and granddaughters, however, looked normal and healthy, not at all unlike the trees she'd grown up around in the habitable zone up in the mountains. Slowly, in fits and starts, but surely, the land was healing.

They'd made it a couple of miles through the ruins of the town and were passing a highway interchange and the remains of what had once been a car lot when Ferrel froze in his tracks and held his fist up, motioning for the rest to do the same. The group circled up and brought their weapons to their shoulders, and Ferrel whispered, "Keep still. Listen."

They did, and after a beat they heard what he had heard: The sound of shuffling feet, at least four pairs of them, skulking around in the brush to their right. The footsteps were slow, random, directionless, and accompanied by no other sound, meaning the source of them hadn't noticed the group yet. But it would be a matter of time.

"Hell," Lilly hissed.

"They don't know we're here yet," Ferrel replied. "I doubt there's gonna be too-too much activity with the lake between us and Atlanta, but I'd still like to avoid any attention. Let's keep moving, but keep it quiet."

They resumed their march, but slower, keeping their weapons up and scanning the trees and collapsing buildings around them. They hadn't gone far, though, when Sean tapped Ferrel's shoulder, pointed down at the roadbed, and hissed, "Oi, Pops, what do you make of that?"

Ferrel motioned for them to stop again and looked down at where his son had pointed. There, at the side of the road, was a bootprint stamped into the dust, and beside it a spent shell casing, shiny and untarnished.

"Huh," he pontificated.

He bent down and picked up the shell casing to examine it. An automatic rifle cartridge, .303 Winchester.

"Well. This prob'ly ain't good."

He was about to get Lilly's attention when there came a burst of rifle fire from the rear of the stack and one of the Ashlanders shouted, "Oi, we got company!"

There were only six, and the Ashlanders had already taken care of it by the time the others turned around, but even lying in the grass with their skulls split open, they were still a frightful enough sight: Human figures long dead with mottled grey skin, stiff joints, sunken eyes. Closer to one of the ruined cities, gunfire out in the wasteland would've been answered at once by a louder chorus of shuffling feet and low, sad moaning; but on the edge of things, with a lake between them and Atlanta, there was only silence.

Ferrel waved Lilly over and pointed out what Sean had found, grumbling, "I don't like that one little bit. None of the regular routes of approach go this way. Weren't expecting anybody out here but us nerds."

Lilly nodded. "I might not think much of this normally, but people who wind up where they aren't supposed to be *and* who shoot Armalite rifles seems a bit much to be a coincidence."

"So what's it mean?" Sean asked.

"Could be loyalists."

A tense silence fell over the group, until Ferrel coughed and growled, "We keep moving. Our first destination is only about seven or eight miles south of here; we can make it before lunchtime if we book it, and if the lake is safe to cross then we can spend the night home free out on one of the islands."

"You sure it'll be safe to be out on the lake when that storm hits?" Lilly asked.

"Might not be too safe to stay on dry land, either, looks like. I'd recommend we take our chances."

They covered the remaining eight miles without incident, moving from the town to a residential suburb to farmland and, finally, a wooded promontory that had once been a campground before the War. Just before lunchtime, as the wind picked up and a light drizzle of rain began to come down, they broke out of the forest of pines and red oaks and finally saw the lake. It was shallow, the view obscured by brakes of willow and cypress and sycamore growing well out into the water, and even in the gathering storm the air was thick with the droning of insects.

"Not much of a lake," Sean said, picking up a stone and tossing it out into the stagnant water. "Looks more like a swamp."

Iris had already doffed her rucksack, and as she rooted through its pockets, she said, "Well, it's not a natural lake, it's a reservoir. The Americans dammed up the Chattahoochee River a few miles southwest of here and flooded the valley to retain water; the islands we're wanting to head for used to be mountaintops. But the dam hasn't been operational in two hundred years, so it's been collecting sediment all this time. It'll be all backed up eventually."

And, with a shout of triumph, she came up holding a Geiger counter and pranced down to the water line, where she threw a probe into the lake, waited a moment, and announced, "It looks safe here. The levels are a bit above normal and, like, I wouldn't wanna drink too much of it, but it's below worrying about."

Lilly clapped her on the shoulder and said, "Alright, then. Everybody, let's take a stop here and do some work."

The ecologists all doffed their rucks and started digging through the pockets. Iris, her eyes sparkling with excitement, took a notebook, a pen, and a canning jar out of her messenger bag and returned to the shore. She filled the jar with still, green water, marked its lid with a letter and number, and jotted down a few notes. Sean watched her work with an easy smile on his face.

As the ecologists took borings from the trees and filled jars with dirt and water, Lilly and Ferrel looked out over the lake. The wind was picking up again, and just beyond the trees they could see the water furled into waves, some of them capping. "Might not be safe to cross after all," Ferrel grumbled, glancing up at the sky.

"Damn shame. If we backtrack and follow the shoreline for a couple of days, that should give us enough data for an initial survey, but you don't know how bad I wanted to check out those islands."

"And you don't know how bad I wanted to crack open that National Guard post. Rotten luck. Maybe the storm will blow itself out while we're walking."

"I sure hope so."

The work was interrupted when the north wind brought with it the sound they'd all been dreading: A chorus of sad, hungry, not-quite-human keening came wafting out of the trees from back the way they'd come. It sounded a few miles off, but right away it was answered by another noise: The steady, crackling tattoo of disciplined automatic rifle fire. The distinct crack and whip of Armalites.

"Well," Ferrel announced.

"That sounded like more than one loyalist."

"Mmhmm. You try and raise base on the radio. We'll get the zodiaks ready."

Back with the rest, the soldiers and ecologists and the other two wasters formed a perimeter while Ferrel and Sean unpacked their rucks, struggling to inflate two black rubber rafts as quickly as possible, while Lilly barked into a handheld radio. They were still only a quick march from the institute, and she was able to make contact right off even through the gathering storm.

"Hey, Baseplate," she sighed, "Mama here. You got your ears on? Over."

"Oh, hey there, Lilly," came a voice on the other end. "You guys okay out there?"

"For now. You guys hear all that shooting?"

"Oh, yeah. We're locking down the facility and I was just about to give you a call. Y'all seen anything?"

"The scavvers found a bootprint and a .303 shell casing on the way in. We haven't seen anybody—well, nobody alive—but Ferrel says he doesn't know of any scavvers making runs out this way. Sounds like loyalists."

"Yikes. They'd be a long-ass way from Ohio, though."

"Well, Kim, special forces are good at covering ground unseen; it's one of the things that makes them special."

"Yeah. So what are y'all gonna do? You need extraction?"

"A minute ago it sounded like they were right behind us. You call Central and ask if they can spare more reinforcements. We're gonna keep going over the lake."

"With the storm coming? Jeez."

"Backtracking right now might be a bad idea."

"Alright. Stay safe and check in whenever you can, yeah?"

"Yeah. Over and out."

Back at the water's edge, Sean and Ferrel had finished inflating the rafts, and the group loaded into them while Ferrel and Cathy argued over a pre-War map of the area, finally agreeing that there looked to be a group of three islands halfway across the lake that they might stand a chance of reaching before the weather got much worse. And the group cast off, the two boats laden with gear and bristling with ready guns like quills on a riled porcupine.

Outside the cover of trees, the wind whipping at their backs furled the lake into frightful white-capping waves, but they came before the wind and rode safely over the crests, not even needing to paddle save to steer the rafts toward the islands that loomed green in the distance, coming ever closer.

Sean, who was crouched at the prow of the foremost boat, had a funny feeling about those islands. He could tell that Cathy and Ferrel, to his left and right, felt it too; a vague sense of worry and unease, that the trees hid some threat which they couldn't quite see. They came on fast, with the wind at their backs, and when they were about a hundred and fifty yards out he spotted a human figure moving amongst the trees. He got Ferrel's attention just as the raft crested another wave and a burst of automatic fire rang out, the distinctive crack and whip of an Armalite. He pulled the trigger of his own rifle and saw a human figure reel within the trees and pitch forward into the water. There came another burst of automatic fire from the island, answered by the crack of Cathy's trail carbine, and then all was silent save for the wind and the waves.

"Aw, mother*fucker*," Ferrel growled.

Sean looked up from his scope and took a look around, and then he heard it too: The hiss of escaping air.

"Anybody hit?" Ferrel asked.

The occupants of both boats appeared to be fine, but the boats themselves were rapidly losing air, bowing over the cresting waves in a sickening way. The islands were still a hundred yards out.

Rowing like hell, they managed to traverse most of the distance before the rafts went down, and there wasn't much swimming left to do; the lake was about hip-deep where the trees stopped. A clap of thunder split the sky and the rain began to come down in earnest as they slogged ashore and took note of the two corpses waiting for them, two middle-aged men who looked to be on the edge of starvation, wearing ragged black campaign shirts with silver eagles embroidered on the collars.

"Get a camp started," Ferrel growled, "and get a fire going. Hurry it up, afore we freeze to death."

The group got to work. Sean found Iris doffing her rucksack and taking off her boots. He offered her his duster and asked, "Hey, are you okay?"

"I'm fine. Are you okay?"

"Yeah. Yeah, I . . . I was just worried about you, is all."

She gave him a quizzical look, then noticed that he was shaking, and not from the cold. She accepted the coat, then threw her arms around and him and said, "Sweetie, please don't try to act tough. Are *you* okay?"

"I . . . I don't know. Iris, I killed a man."

"No, you didn't. You killed a fascist."

He laughed. "Yeah. Yeah, I guess you're right."

"I'm always right. But if you need to talk, you're with good people, alright?"

"Yeah."

Under a tarp and around the beginnings of a campfire, the group took council on the day's events while the thunderstorm raged around them. Cathy growled, "Can't fucking believe there's boneheads this far south."

The Ashlander commissar shrugged. "Most of the Arditi refused to demobilize after the war. We've run them out of Ohio and now they're sneaking off into whatever forgotten corners and holes in the walls they can still hide in. And there ain't no bigger hole in the wall than Atlanta."

"Yeah, I guess you're right. Still, of all the rotten luck, huh?"

"This ain't good," Ferrel grumbled. "I remember the war after Columbus fell. I was part of the big final push into Cleveland when we put the boots to Jimmy Stockdale. When these fuckers get desperate, they get mean. If there's more of 'em hiding out around here, they'll be after us."

"Looks like we're safe for now, between the storm and the isolation. But speaking of the isolation, I would like to know how in the hell we plan to get off this goddamn island."

"I dunno," Iris said, "that part seems like it'd be the easy part."

"I'm all ears, sister."

"Well, these are good pollard trees. This island is all loblolly and eastern white pine, and they're nice and straight, and there's a lot of 'em."

"Huh?"

"We all brought rope, right?"

"Well, yeah."

And Iris reached across to the far side of her rucksack, dropped her felling axe out of its sheath, and laid it across her lap. "Well, we're foresters. We brought tools."

II.

The storm only got worse through the afternoon and showed no signs of slacking until evening. The group changed into dry clothes and spent the day huddled around their fire dishing out hot chow—the concentrated and fortified plant proteins that the Ashlanders shipped down in 20-kilo sacks of white powder, like cocaine from Kentucky; it tasted like nothing, but it ate—and arguing while a few unlucky souls in groups of three went out to watch their perimeter every few minutes. Sean and Iris huddled close to each other, trying and failing to stay dry, trying and mostly succeeding to stay warm, oblivious to the misery around them as they luxuriated in each other's company and talked on and on about not much at all.

By early evening, the rain slackened just enough to give them a couple of hours of clear daylight, and the ecologists got to work picking out a few tall, straight trees and bringing them down. Iris, as small as she was, seemed a natural at it, swinging her massive axe in a practiced, easy rhythm, notching one side of a tree and hewing out the other so that, within the span of just a few minutes, the sixty-foot Georgia pine came crashing down exactly where she'd meant it to. Sean stood by and watched her for a while, his face glowing with respect and admiration and not a little boyish arousal, but decided to find himself something productive to do. He, like his father, was an anarchist, and would've called himself a feminist, but he still felt some kind of a way about watching his girlfriend work harder than he ever had in his life without breaking a sweat. As he walked off, he shook those thoughts out of his head, internally berating himself for how silly they sounded. He brought his rifle to low ready and headed for the shore, intending to walk the perimeter, and as he went he thought that Iris must be the only person on Earth who could make felling a tree seem graceful, and he fantasized about rubbing the knots out of her muscles when they bedded down for the night.

As he slunk through the trees around the edge of the island, rifle in hand, something white caught Sean's eye in the dying light. He stopped, took a second look, and found himself staring into the empty eyes of a grinning human skull nestled in the crook of a red oak. A long, cruel combat knife jutted out of the tree's trunk just below the skull's jagged teeth. Both looked reasonably fresh.

He made his way back to the others at a jog and found Ferrel and the political commissar sitting around the fire having a spirited discussion that seemed to mainly consist of them quoting old dead men at each other. He jogged up to them and panted, "Alright. You two, just the two I was looking for. I, uh . . . found something."

"What did you want them for?" Ferrel asked, gesturing at the commissar.

"You'll see. Just follow me. I, uh . . . I found something."

The two of them followed him back to the shore and back to the tree, which they stood observing in silence until Ferrel at last spat on the ground and said, "Well."

"That could mean a lot of things," the commissar said, "and none of them are good. The death's-head and dagger was the sign and seal of the Arditi back during the war, and the loyalists still cling to it just like they do everything else."

"Hey, red," Ferrel grumbled, pointing at the base of the tree, "what do you make of that one?"

Sean and the commissar both looked, and saw a symbol gouged into the trunk. It was a circle with radial spokes, like a wagon wheel, and the spokes were jagged like lightning bolts. It looked fresh. The commissar kicked the symbol, grinding the heel of their boot into the bark, and said, "Yeah, if it didn't look like boneheads before—and it did—it sure as shit does now."

"That's one of them spooky mystical symbols, though," Ferrel said. "The Blacklanders were falangists; hella Catholic. Only a special kind of bonehead would put that there." And he looked back up at the skull, studying it closely, and after a beat his eyes went wide and he snatched it out of the tree.

"What's up, Pops?" Sean asked.

Ferrel passed the skull to the commissar. It felt heavy, much heavier than it should've been, and unnaturally cold. And its canines were longer than normal, tapering into sharp, fearsome points.

"Well, *fuck me*," they growled.

Sean rolled his eyes. "Do either one of y'all wanna tell me what the hell it is I found?"

"Kid, this ain't just some weird loyalist war totem. I think you found an altar."

The three of them returned to the camp, and Ferrel spotted Cathy sitting by the fire. He cried out, "Oi, waster! Catch!" and tossed her the skull.

Cathy caught the skull in the air, and at once threw it to the ground with a cry of disgust and barked, "Jesus fucking Christ, Ferrel! Where the hell did you find that thing?"

"My boy found it, walkin the perimeter. Found it tucked into an oak tree with a Black Sun carved into it."

"Ferrel, that's a goddamn hunter's skull."

"Mmhmm. And the sun's almost down. Y'all seen Lilly?"

"She's right over there, about to check in with base on the radio. Oi! Miz Lilly! The kid found somethin!"

Lilly came trotting over with Iris at her heels, and they explained to her what Sean had found. Her face went grey, and she muttered, "Oh, Lord. Oh, this ain't good."

"Fascists are bad enough," Ferrel grumbled, "and hunters are bad enough, and we're stuck on this shitty little island with no boats and some kinda loyalist religious fanatics skulking around in the dark."

"And we merc'd two of 'em on the way in and fucked up

their special tree and camped out on their special island. And we're *trapped* on that island."

"We'll have a raft ready before lunchtime tomorrow," Iris said. "A damned good one, too."

"Lunchtime tomorrow is a long, long way away, baby." And Lilly sighed and shook her head and said, "Set a double watch. *At least* four rifles on duty at all times, no less, till the sun comes up. And the rest of us should settle in and try to get some sleep. I reckon we're gonna need it."

———

The night came on slowly, and passed slower. Ever since the War—not the war with the fascists a few years previous, but the War, the War two centuries before that, when atomic fire rained from the sky and Old America burned—the exclusion zones around the big cities had always been havens of death, and not just the death that poisoned the air and water and soil and made the trees grow all wrong. Some kinds of death walked on two legs.

There were the roamers, the people who'd gotten sick and got better wrong, some Old American weapon that had gotten out of control and turned people into mindless, moaning hordes of grasping hands and gnashing teeth. But small groups of roamers were easy to kill, and any good waster would know how to avoid the large groups. Ever since folks really started settling down in the habitable zones beyond the mountains, roamers were more of a nuisance than a threat, inconveniencing wasters and ecologists outside of old car lots.

The same could not be said for hunters.

The other kind of death, the one that only came out at night and moved silently in groups of two or three, was the one that scavvers and soldiers talked about in hushed whispers around their campfires. They looked human, at a glance, but they moved faster than a human should and could soak up bullets like a sponge. Few people had ever seen a hunter, and fewer still had fought one and lived to talk about it, and most of the time the only sign that a pair of hunters had passed through an area would be a neatly dismembered corpse, or a home made empty, or a team of scavengers heading out into the wasteland and not coming back.

Hunters were little understood, but folks knew that they were an old menace, older than the roamers, older than the War, a relic of a much darker past that should never have persisted into the modern world. And they knew that, in some type of a way, the hunters and the human warlords who still dreamed of Old America tended to get along more than they didn't.

So the expedition circled tight around their campfire, and set a double watch, and waited for dawn, trying to sleep and sleeping little. Sean and Iris stayed close to each other, spending most of the night in each other's arms, but within the same perimeter as the others; contrary to Ferral's fears, they were certainly horny, but they weren't stupid. After an abortive attempt at sleep, they spent their night sitting up and talking, stealing quick tender kisses when they thought no-one could see. Everyone, of course, saw.

Ferrel and Cathy sat together on the other side of the fire. She managed, after a struggle, to light one of her damp cigarettes, and she took a long drag, pointed over her shoulder to where the kids sat under Sean's duster, and said, "Them two are too goddamn cute, man."

Ferrel's perpetual frown curled up around its edges, a tick that Cathy recognized as Ferrel's equivalent of a wide, warm smile, and he lit his own smoke and grumbled, "Mmhmm. It's good to see the kids so happy. Hell, he reminds me of what I was like back when I met his mama."

"Aw, hell, Ferrel, I didn't know you was a married man."

"Used to be. Ain't been for a while. War."

Cathy squeezed his shoulder and gave him a sympathetic nod; they had all lost someone. After a beat, she added, "That girl, she's like me, y'know?"

"Mmhmm."

"I can see he treats her right."

"He fuckin better, if he knows what's good for him."

"Y'know, Ferrel, you're an asshole, but you seem like a pretty good dad."

"I fuckin hope so. It's the least I can do, and the least he deserves. I love that boy to pieces, y'know. And that girl is one the smartest people I ever met, and she's got a good heart.

My opinion may not be worth a dried turd, but I do approve of her."

"Yeah, she seems alright for an authoritarian."

Just after midnight, Cathy and Ferrel and two of the soldiers stood on the shoreline, watching the lake's surface as best they could through the haze of rain as the storm picked back up. They were all four seasoned veterans, blooded professionals, and they could feel a threat out in the darkness even if they couldn't see it. As they made their rounds, they would turn away from the island, scan the darkened trees and the raging lake beyond them, and continue on their way, cursing the wind and rain.

After their third circuit of the island, near the spot where Sean had found the skull a few hours previously, they were about to head back to camp and wake up their relief when one of the Ashlanders at last spotted something. On the shore in front of them, neatly stamped into the mud and quickly washing away in the rain, was a bootprint, and not one of theirs.

"Oh, *Hell*," Ferrel hissed.

As they turned to run back to the camp, a burst of rifle fire split the night air and thumped into a tree a few inches from Cathy's head. The four of them threw themselves to the ground and returned fire blindly into the darkness. Night-blind from rain and from muzzle flash, they saw nothing, but a few seconds of silence passed and Cathy hissed, "We didn't even fucking see them."

"Mmhmm," Ferrel pontificated.

"Cover me. I'm gonna bound."

She started to lift herself up, and the movement was met at once by another burst of rifle fire slamming into the mud where her head had been a second before. They answered again, and were rewarded by a cry of agony and the sound of something heavy hitting the ground. Cathy bounded toward the source of the sound, ducked behind a tree after sprinting a few yards, and almost tripped over a man lying in the mud and clutching a ragged, bloody hole in his stomach, trying to hide. He had the same haggard, desperate, starving look as the two they'd run into on the way in, but was several years older, and rather than a ragged combat uniform he wore a set of tattered black robes. She held him there in the mud and barked, "Oi! I got a fucking war cleric over here!"

"You will *suffer* for defiling this place," the man on the ground hissed.

One of the Ashlanders got to them first, and without a word he pushed Cathy away and punched the bleeding war cleric in the face.

"Dude," she asked, cocking an eyebrow, "what the fuck?"

The Ashlander ignored her. He struck the war cleric again and growled, "Alright, padre, time to start talking."

"You are all going to die," the war cleric groaned. "You

are all going to suffer and die for defiling this place, and you especially, you godless effeminate Bolshevist coward."

The Ashlander smirked. He undid the top of his flecktarn blouse and pulled it down just enough to reveal a tattoo on his chest just below the collarbone. It was of a crossed-out swastika, though the hashing was a bit off-center and the swastika itself was badly faded, indicating that the crossing out was a much later addition.

"Fucking *renegade!*" The war cleric spat the word, as though it tasted foul.

"Fucking loyalist. Start talking and you might live through the night."

"You won't."

"What are you doing here? How many more are out there?"

"You have defiled Her sanctum, traitor. She will not be pleased. She is coming, and She will expect Her sacrifice."

"What's the move, padre? We ain't Catholic anymore?"

The war cleric drew in a long, ragged breath, and pink foam bubbled up at the corners of his mouth. With a harsh, painful laugh, he said, "The false God abandoned us at the hour of truth. We have found new gods, and better. Gods of iron and blood."

"How many more are out here?"

"You'll find out soon enough, traitor."

And the war cleric let out a last ragged, rattling breath, and did not speak again. After a beat, Cathy clapped the

Ashlander on the shoulder and said, "Damn, Eddie, I didn't know you was a renegade."

"Well, it ain't something I like to talk about much."

"Hey, you know Jules Binachi, right?"

"Of course. I mean, I never met her, but every renegade knows Jules Binachi. That's like asking a priest if he knows Jesus Christ."

"That ecologist girl is Jules Binachi's apprentice."

"No shit? Wow, what a small world."

Ferrel cleared his throat and grumbled, "So about the situation at hand."

"Yeah. I fucking hate war clerics, man, and apparently they found a way to get even weirder."

"Whatcha think he was talkin about?"

"Hell all I know, brother. I—wait. Oh, Hell."

Eddie gestured at the dead war cleric's neck. It was covered in scars, each scar a pair of twin pinpricks, rather like snakebites.

"Well," Ferrel mused, "this ain't good."

The four of them stood up and started to head back toward camp when the night was split again by more rifle fire from the interior of the island, and another volley answering it. A proper firefight was underway.

Sean couldn't see shit.

Night-blind from muzzle flash, half-blind from the rain in his eyes, trying to glass the darkened forest through a quickly fogging scope, he fired into the dark at foes he couldn't see, trying his best to focus in on movement, hoping he might at least help keep them pinned down. Iris lay prone beside him, doing the same with her Kalashnikov, though hers had iron sights and she could at least see a bit better. He kept his focus downrange, but his thoughts were hectic, wandering between *She's in the middle of this* and *My dad's out there.*

He guessed there must be about six or seven raiders out in the dark, meaning his side had the greater number, and if these were loyalists then they were probably tired and starving and desperate; it had been a good few years since their Republic fell. Why would they pick a fight that they had to know they couldn't win?

And he remembered the skull, and shuddered. Most likely they had help.

A cry of desperate rage erupted from the darkness, and for the first time Sean got a good look at his enemy: A middle-aged man in a tattered black button-up shirt rushed out of the trees toward them, swinging an empty Armalite rifle like a club and roaring like a lion. He was riddled with bullets and slumped dead to the ground.

A burst of rifle fire caught one of the Ashlanders in the chest, and another felled one of the ecologists, but the counterfire ceased and six more blackshirts came running out of the darkness, bellowing rage with murder in their eyes. They didn't last long.

In the silence that followed, the night seemed to grow darker, colder, and the group felt an icy knot of fear settle into each of their bellies. Most of them—including Sean and Iris—looked around, confused, not sure what to make of this pall of fear that had settled over them like fog, not sure what it was that they were afraid of. But the old hands tightened their grips on their rifles and did not move. Seeing that, Sean guessed what was coming.

Another figure emerged from the darkness and into view. She did not run, but came toward them at an easy stroll, like a woman walking through a park. A few people opened fire as soon as she came into view; she took the rounds in the torso, staggered, recovered, kept walking. Fear radiated from her like a miasma, growing stronger as she came closer, and as she strolled into view two of the ecologists screamed and dashed away into the darkness.

At last, she came close enough for Sean to get a real look at her. She was tall and fair, with toned, wiry muscles and a long, noble face topped by a head of flaxen hair slicked back with rain. She might've looked like a marble statue given life if not for her eyes, which were solid black and soulless with no discernable whites, and for her clothes; the strange woman wore the tattered remains of a black muslin bodice and hoop skirt, an outfit that might've looked lovely and fair at some point in the depths of the past.

She smiled a rictus, humorless smile, showing off her canines, far too long and ending in needle points.

Another burst of rifle fire punched into her chest, and again she staggered, recovered, and kept walking. Through the rips in her bodice, Sean watched the entrance wounds stitch themselves closed. She stretched out her arm, and another waster screamed and ran.

"You have defiled my hermitage," she said in a chill voice that thickened the pall of terror and sparked more flight, or rooted the rest of them in fear. Her accent was strange, foreign, difficult to place, as though she'd come from a faraway part of the world, or spoke from some distant point in time.

"You have trespassed upon my place of rest. At long last I found servants, and you have murdered them. What shall I do with you? I will feed. *I--"*

There was another burst of rifle fire from just to Sean's right, from Iris. The burst struck the creature not in the chest, but in the head, blowing away a piece of her skull and sending her reeling backwards. She recovered far more slowly, struggling to pull herself up to her knees, and it almost broke the spell, but as she reeled and struggled she let out an ear-splitting howl that hurt to listen to; Sean was sure he'd go deaf, and just managed to stop himself from dropping his rifle to clamp his hands over his ears. He fired again, but his hands shook terribly and the shot went wild, thumping into a tree somewhere out in the darkness. The woman pulled herself up to her feet and came striding forward, toward him. He jumped to his feet and backpedaled, trying to work the bolt of his rifle. It was stuck fast, soaked with rain and choked with sand. He backed up hard into a tree, and looking around he saw that only he and Lilly remained. The rest had fled.

The creature headed right for him. Lilly stepped in front of her; casually, like opening a door, she gave Lilly a shove and sent her reeling to the ground as though she'd been struck by a boxer. Sean managed to clear the jam, but she was on top of him within three strides, grabbing him by the front of his shirt and lifting him into the air as though he weighed nothing. Her dead, black eyes were terrible, and her breath smelled like blood, and the hideous wound in her head was healing slowly and leaked viscous black ichor.

"*You,*" she growled. "*I will hunt the others at my leisure, but you . . . you are the bravest. You will taste the sweetest.*"

The creature opened her mouth, baring her canines, and moved to sink them into his neck. But the bite never came.

A loud, low *thunk!* sounded from just behind her, and her face froze, and she dropped him into a heap in the mud. She collapsed to the ground beside him with a double-bit felling axe jutting from the back of her head.

The creature groaned, twitching like a dying spider, trying to lift herself up on her elbows. Iris put a boot on her back, freed the axe, and brought it down again, and again, and again until the creature's head was an oozing pulp and her limbs no longer twitched. Through the whole affair, Iris growled under her breath in time with the falling axe; Sean couldn't quite make out the words, save for three repeated again and again: "*. . . . my . . . fucking . . . boyfriend . . .*"

Sean stared up at her, his terror melting away into awe, almost reverence. She rested the axe on her shoulder and said, "We should go check on Miss Lilly. I think she might be concussed."

He caught his breath and muttered, "Uh . . . yeah. Yeah."

She helped him to his feet just as Ferrel and the others made it back to the camp. The old scavenger froze at the sight in front of him, and he looked back and forth between the headless hunter and the axe dripping with ichor and asked, "You take care of that yourself?"

"Uh-huh."

"Everybody else get spooked?"

"Lilly's still here. She might have got hurt, but I think she'll be okay."

"Well, I'll be goddamned. I'm impressed, kid. You got cooler nerves than a lot of veteran wasters."

Iris leaned her axe against a tree and shrugged. "I'm a scientist, Mr. Ferrel."

4: WEREWOLF

**[AD 2263, 198 years post-War;
somewhere in Pennsylvania]**

Trip couldn't remember the last time he'd had a
decent meal.

As the group made camp in the crumbling husk of what
had once been an Olive Garden, the night's chow made him
wonder if he'd be better off staying hungry: They'd put
together one pound of that weird powdered tofu shit the
Ashlanders used for field rations, a handful of nuts, and a
tumorous feral dog. The captain was a decent enough chef,
but even a proper artist could only do so much with the mate-
rials on hand, and when supper was dished out the captain
handed him a tin cup of brown slop with a chunk of grey
meat floating in it. It smelled like an open septic tank.

"What the fuck is this shit?" Trip inquired.

"It's food," the captain growled. "There something wrong with it, lance corporal?"

"Yeah, a couple things."

"If you don't like it, don't fucking eat it."

Trip shrugged; this would be his first meal in two days. He held his nose, forced the concoction down his throat in two quick gulps, and managed not to vomit. After recovering, he wiped his mouth and asked, "Did those commies have any goddamn cigarettes?"

"Don't know," the captain grumbled. "Why don't you go check?"

Trip rolled his eyes, got up, and sauntered to the far side of their camp. That afternoon, they'd found the Olive Garden occupied by a scavenger expedition, a mix of Ashlander soldiers in flecktarn uniforms and Freesider wasteland rangers in long blank dusters, and all the godless Bolshevists now lay stacked up in a neat little pile in the corner, growing cold and adding to the cornucopia of fascinating smells. The lance corporal dug around through the dead scavvers' backpacks and pockets until he found a book of matches and a pack of cigarettes. He lit a smoke, reclined against the pile, and contemplated his lot in life: When he'd passed stormptrooper selection at 17, a year before Columbus fell, he hadn't been sure what further military service held for him, but it certainly hadn't been this. He wondered how his dad and sisters were faring in Dayton, after two years of commie occupation. Now, at 20, he was a stay-behind operative starving to death on the outskirts of Pittsburgh. Life, he thought, sure takes us places.

The cigarettes were Ashlander cigarettes, and the smell of good Kentucky tobacco filling the Olive Garden summoned the rest of the group over to the pile, disturbing Trip's repose as they rooted around amongst the corpses for prizes of their own. The signalman, a shifty little man who gave Trip the spooks, kicked one of them and said, "Man, there's some fine-lookin girls in this woodpile. Damn shame we couldn't take one of 'em alive."

"I'd be careful with that," the captain said. "You never can tell with these degenerates. Might just pull down her pants and find a little surprise between her legs."

"Boss, at this point, I'll fuckin take what I can get. Ass is ass."

The group burst into hearty laughter at that, and the signalman added, "Hell, if we keep eating all this goddamn Kentucky soy for much longer, we might start lookin real pretty our own selves. You say they got chow in Vermont?"

"Yeah, they got chow in Vermont. We're about a month out."

"Shit. What are we gonna eat for a month?"

"Soy powder, dead dog, and pine nuts. And, if you keep fuckin whining, signalman."

The signalman found a bag of jerky in one of the Ashlanders' pockets, and as he slunk off into the darkness to go enjoy it, he socked Trip in the shoulder and cackled, "Hey, kid, if you start feelin' estrogenated, lemme know."

Trip pretended to laugh at the joke, but there was a dark look in the signalman's eyes, a hungry look. It made Trip wonder which the signalman would rather be doing: Fucking him or eating him. He supposed it was probably both.

"Hey, captain," he said, lighting another smoke, "what's our marching orders for tomorrow?"

"Need to get over the river," the captain replied. "We'll avoid the worst of the exclusion zone by going north a ways to the railway bridge. Once we're past Pittsburgh, we'll be outta the worst of it and just picking our way through the woods. Should get easy after tomorrow."

"The hell are we gonna eat, though?"

"Shut the fuck up."

Trip shut the fuck up. From behind him, he heard one of the rag-pickers—the automatic rifleman—growl with rage and call out, "Hey, boss, look what we fuckin got here."

The group came over to look. One of the corpses wore a black button up campaign shirt with silver eagles embroidered on the collar, same as theirs, but his black shirt had had the sleeves cut off and was covered in patches. The automatic rifleman rolled him over and confirmed their suspicions: The word "RENEGADE" was spread across the back of it in big block letters.

"Fucking traitor," the captain hissed. "Drag his ass outside. Maybe he'll poison the dogs."

They'd all heard the stories about the Renegades: Arditi stormtroopers who'd forsworn their oaths and gone over to the reds during the war. Those who'd remained loyal to the cause would never forgive them for it, but Trip couldn't help but notice that the dead Renegade they were dragging outside looked like he'd been eating pretty well.

The dead Renegade did not, in fact, poison the dogs, though it wasn't for a lack of trying. When Trip walked out onto the darkened street for his watch shift roundabouts 0200, there was nothing left of the traitor but a few scraps of fabric and an ugly red stain on the concrete, leading deeper into the ruined, crumbling city with its collapsing towers looming like dead gods in the darkness. He found himself thinking about Old America a lot; growing up, he'd heard stories about how it was a beautiful dream, a country where white men fleeing the iniquities of European Jewry had subdued the lesser, barbarous races and built a powerful, Christian nation, only to be undone by their own permissive degeneracies. But, looking at the rotting office towers looming over the Olive Garden, Trip counted his ribs and thought that he didn't believe he'd ever actually met a Jew, European or otherwise, and that the Old Americans probably ate something besides sick, dead dog every other night. There hadn't been any Old Americans around to ask for about 200 years, but from context clues he reckoned they ate olives.

Trip slung his battle rifle and stuck his hands in his pockets as he paced around the block, not paying particular attention to much of anything. The dogs were unlikely to come too close to a building that smelled so strongly of people, and any other kind of death that the wasteland held— the death that walked on two legs—would be unavoidable anyways. His belly rumbled again, and his black shirt—which had once fit like a glove but was now at least a size too big— fluttered in the wind, and he reckoned that maybe getting killed wouldn't be so bad. At least *somebody* would get a decent meal out of it.

He looked down at his shirt, which was filthy, tattered, greying in places, and thought about how proud his dad had been to see him in it, and how the black shirt and skull tattoo had bought him instant respect from other men and instant desirability from girls once he'd made lance corporal and finally passed selection; a heady thing for a 17-year-old from Dayton who barely knew how to read. It hadn't lasted long. Almost the moment he'd donned his fine new uniform, the war with the commies down south heated up again, and the war went bad, then went worse, until at last the stormtroopers —what few of them hadn't already surrendered or already gotten themselves shot—received two conflicting sets of orders: The man in Cleveland said to stand down and demo- bilize, while the man who'd fled to Vermont said to kick off the stay-behind operation. Operation Werewolf, they called it. A guerrilla war against the godless communist occupation of the Blackland New Republic.

News wasn't exactly easy to come by in the exclusion zone, but Trip only knew of five or six operating groups who'd actually gone out to commence Operation Werewolf, and only knew of about three—including his—that were still operating. And with all of the captain's talk of giving up their less-than-successful campaign of manhunting and sabotage to pull up stakes and run for Vermont, he reckoned you could drop that number down to two. All his life, from his dad and the officers and the war clerics, Trip had heard horror story after horror story about the unspeakable things that the godless Bolshevists liked to do to their prisoners, but all the newly-minted reds in Renegade cuts strolling around the wasteland nowadays made him feel some kind of a way about all of that.

Walking around to the side of the Olive Garden, where the firefight had begun earlier in the day, Trip rolled his eyes and announced to God and nobody, "Well, Trip Donahue, I reckon you might have made some poor life choices."

When he came to the spot where the operating group had commenced its glorious victory over an unsuspecting band of drunk and stoned wasteland scavengers, evinced by the brass littering the pavement and the bullet holes in the wall, he spotted something that had gone unnoticed during the sweep. Tossed aside and forgotten in the underbrush that filled the dying city lay a handheld 2-way radio. An Ashlander's radio.

Assuming it still had some battery life left, it would be encrypted and tuned to one of the reds' military frequencies. He stood staring at it for a few eternities, listening to his belly rumble, before he took a cautious look around and walked over to pick it up.

"Uhh . . . All call signs, all call signs, commo check, repeat, commo check, over."

There was a tense, disappointing silence that dragged on into awkwardness before a quiet, tinny voice responded, "Yeah, you're a little fuzzy, but I hear ya, buddy. Whatcha got? Over."

Trip didn't say anything; he hadn't planned this far ahead. After another awkward silence, the voice crackled, "What's your call sign, cowpoke? Over."

"Uhh . . . This is Werewolf 6. Over."

The silence that followed dragged on for a full few minutes, and Trip was about to throw the radio down and walk away when a different voice came over the line, a woman's voice dripping with authority and with anger, growling, "Werewolf 6, this is Crow 9. What the fuck do you want, boot boy?"

"Yeah," Trip said, taking a seat on the pavement, "hear that loud and clear, Crow 9. Listen, uh . . . is it too late to surrender? Over."

"Oh, ho-ly shit. Yeah, you're a *bit* late to the party, Were-wolf 6; about two fucking years late. I—Kid, how old are you? Over."

"Uhh . . . I'm 20, ma'am."

"Jesus fucking Christ. Okay, talk to me, kid. Who the hell are you? Who are you with? Where are y'all at? Gimme something and maybe we can talk. Over."

"Okay. Uhh . . . Can I ask who I'm talking to? Over."

"Ramirez, political officer, Ashland's Department of Intelligence and Security; AKA the only person you're likely to get who might can make you a deal. Now gimme something."

"Okay. Um . . . The name's Trip Donahue, lance corporal, fifth special operations group, charlie company, first assault, first infantry. Currently bivouacked just outside of Pittsburgh. Uh, over."

"How many boneheads in your group, kid?"

"Six, including me. We're heading out to Vermont tomorrow morning."

"Alright, alright, we might be onto something. Kid, how did you get on this channel? Over."

"I, uh . . . I found a radio."

"*Chinga* . . . Alright, sure. So you say you've finally got some quit in you?"

"Look, man, I . . . I didn't sign up for whatever the fuck this is, I ain't had a decent meal in months, I'm pretty sure my signalman wants to fuck me or eat me or fuckin eat me . . . Whatever you bolshies plan on doing with us, I don't fuckin care. You can rip out my fingernails and throw me in a gulag or what the fuck ever as long as there's food. This is bullshit. This is all a bunch of bullshit."

"It sure is, kid. Listen: You said the name's Trip?"

"Yeah, Trip Donahue."

"Listen to me, Trip. You are a little bit late to the party; that offer for y'all to stand down and demobilize after the war was a one-time deal. We ain't gonna give you the full Jules Binachi treatment, but I think I can make you an offer. If you give me a little something to show me you mean it, I can at least promise you that you'll slip the noose. How does that sound? Over."

"I'll fuckin take whatever you got, ma'am. Over."

"You can call me Lynn, Trip. Now, talk to me. Do you know what part of Pittsburgh you're in? And how y'all are planning on getting from there to Vermont?"

Trip walked back into the restaurant a few minutes later, unable to hide the spring in his step. When he found the next watchman and kicked him awake, the signalman looked up at him and sneered, "What the fuck are you so happy about, you little faggot?"

"I'm happy to finally go the fuck back to bed," Trip replied. "You got next watch, man."

"Yeah, yeah. I'm up, I'm up."

Trip walked over to his own bedroll and reclined against

the wall, lighting one of his cigarettes and reveling in the smell and taste of good Kentucky tobacco. After getting up, the signalman walked over and said, "Kid, I ain't gonna lie. I'm pretty worried about the next few days. I dunno if we got enough food to make it all the way to fuckin Vermont."

"Looks that way. You want somethin?"

"Yeah, kid. I been thinking. I hear they got a good setup over there in Vermont, towns and guns and shit, and food. But a month is a long fuckin time, man. We ain't gonna make it, going on like this. If the captain knew where some chow was, he woulda moved us toward it a long time ago."

"Yeah, I reckon."

"I dunno about you, kid, but I ain't gonna die out here. I ain't. Listen: We're warriors, right? That's what these black shirts and skull tattoos are supposed to mean; we're *warriors*, just like in old times. We're the werewolves."

"Sure, dude."

"Well, listen, kid: I got an idea. There's a great big pile of red meat just sitting over there. Bolshie has gotta taste better than dog, right?"

"I, uh . . . I think I'm good, dude."

"Suit yourself, kid. But I ain't fuckin dying out here. I ain't."

The signalman turned and made his way over to the woodpile. Trip didn't get much sleep that night.

The next day dawned blue and clear, and the trail northeast took them through what had once been a residential suburb. They walked through a sprawling landscape of ruined houses and driveways overgrown with hardwoods and verdant foliage that would've been beautiful under any other circumstances, but the filthy, starving blackshirts advancing in an infantry wedge as they watched out for signs of wasteland scavengers took little notice of the greenery. The spring in Trip's step was gone, and he trembled with nerves as the group moved north and approached the river. The only one who seemed to have gotten any rest during the night was the signalman, but Trip tried not to think about that too much. He scanned the trees and the buildings religiously, like a new recruit just learning about situational awareness; he didn't know what he was expecting to happen, but he knew it would be big, and he knew it would be soon. He knew that the rest of the group was just as fried as he was, that his obvious nerves were shared by everyone at some level or other, but he couldn't help thinking that they could see treason in his eyes, in the way his hands shook as he cradled his Armalite. But all of their hands were shaking just as much, from thirst and exhaustion and hunger. All of them except for the signalman.

They didn't stop for lunch, with no chow to dish out, but around noon they reached a set of railroad tracks running north to south where they could just see the wide, brown Ohio River ahead of them through the trees, and the captain motioned for them to stop and circle up. He pointed northeast, toward the river, where they could just see the tip of an island far away and almost make out the span of a railway bridge running across it and, he whispered, "We're almost home free, boys. Once we get across, we'll be too far east for the reds to give us any trouble. I ain't seen any sign of pursuit, but that nest of freaks we burned out yesterday might have had themselves some friends; and the closer we get to the city center, the more likely we are to run into roamers. Let's not get complacent. I'm not gonna lie, I got a bad feeling about today, and I been doin this long enough to trust those feelings."

The group nodded, and the captain said, "Me and Stockdale are gonna head straight to the railway bridge. Maxwell, Wingfield, you two head back the way we came a ways and then loop northeast. We'll rendezvous at the bridge."

The automatic rifleman and the grenadier got up, checked their weapons, and headed off into the woods without another word.

As the captain got up, he pointed at Trip and the signalman and said, "Covington, Donahue, you two sit tight here for five minutes and then follow me and Stockdale north to the rendezvous point. If y'all run into trouble, you know what to do."

Trip felt a cold knot of fear tightening in his belly. The signalman gave a jaunty salute and said, "Will do, boss."

"Don't salute officers in the field, you goddamn moron."

When they were alone together, Trip kept his eyes on the

signalman and prayed—he wasn't sure to who—that whatever was about to happen would hurry up and happen. The signalman leaned against a tree and said, "Fuckin relax, kid. The boss is just paranoid; there ain't no reds around for miles. You got any smokes left?"

Trip thought about the combat knife hanging from his belt. He wondered if he'd be able to move fast enough to close the distance before the signalman could swing his Armalite back up. He decided against it; his adversary was the one who'd gone to bed with a full belly. With a sigh, he fished the pack out of his pocket and said, "Yeah, man. It's our lucky day; I got two left."

"Killer. Let's us share a toast before we strike out for freedom."

As they lit up, Trip wracked his brain trying to remember the instructions that the nice lady on the radio had given him. He unbuttoned his campaign shirt, baring the pasty white skin on his chest and belly between the tattoos, and muttered, "Fuckin hot out today, yeah?"

"Hotter, with you showing a little skin."

Trip rolled his eyes. The signalman laughed and asked, "Kid, what the hell are you so nervous about? Chill."

Trip sighed again and turned to take another look at the trees, desperately willing whatever was about to happen to hurry up and happen. When he turned back around, the signalman was gone.

He felt the cold knot of fear in his gut rise up into panic, felt a hundred unseen eyes watching him through the trees, and before he could run off or look around he felt something poke him between the shoulderblades and heard the signalman hiss, "Relax, kid. No sudden moves, alright?"

Panting, shaking, Trip raised his hands and muttered, "Yeah, man. Yeah. Sure."

"You know what's about to happen, right?"

"I, ah . . . I think I can guess."

"I knew you wasn't as dumb as you look. Get on your knees."

Trip complied, and he felt the barrel of an Armalite press into the back of his head as the signalman said, "You know we're way beyond good and evil out here, kid. Nobody likes you and nobody gives a fuck what happens to you; the captain's gonna take whatever I tell him. Now, it's a hell of a long way to Vermont, we ain't got enough chow, and *you* get to decide which of the two most basic human desires I'm gonna satisfy on the way there. So you do what I say if you don't wanna grow an extra hole in your head. You tracking?"

He closed his eyes and prayed harder, though he wasn't sure to who, as he heard the sound of a fly unzipping. "Yeah, man. Sure, man."

"Good girl. You could pass for one, y'know, you scrawny little fuck. Makes things easier for me. Now turn around."

Trip froze, unable to comply, fight, or fly as every muscle in his body tensed and seized. The signalman kicked him in the back, sending him sprawling out on his face, and grumbled, "Alright then, if you don't wanna be a good girl, we can do it the hard way."

He clenched his teeth and willed himself not to make a sound, too terrified to fight back but determined to retain some shred of dignity. But the indignity never came. He'd only been on the ground for half a second when he heard gunshots ring out from somewhere off to the north. Disciplined pairs of automatic fire. And he recognized the sound: Kalashnikovs.

"What in the--" the signalman barked.

Trip moved, then. He rolled over to see the signalman looking away, toward the north, his attention turned elsewhere for the moment. Desperate, with a sound that was meant to be a battle cry but came out as a high, warbling moan, he grabbed the signalman's rifle by the barrel and pulled as hard as he could, sending it sailing out into the trees where it struck something solid and slap-fired, filling the air with the distinctive .303 Winchester report. And, just as the signalman began to react, the combat knife came out. Trip was, it turned out, fast enough to close the gap after all.

***

Trip Donahue didn't know how long he spent kneeling over the signalman's broken body, his breath ragged, his heart pounding in his ears. He told himself he was trying to catch his breath, but he knew he couldn't get up if he tried. He didn't look up as the shooting picked up to the north and then to the west, didn't look up when the shooting stopped, didn't look up as he heard footsteps approaching through the brush; he finally did look up when a woman's voice—one he recognized—barked, "Alright, kid, put the knife down."

Four people, two men and two women in flecktarn combat fatigues, stood nearby, staring at him down the sights of their Kalashnikovs. He dropped his combat knife, and one of the soldiers—a small woman with brown skin, black hair, big coke-bottle glasses, and a killer's eyes—asked, "So you're Lance Corporal Trip Donahue, right?"

"Y--yes, ma'am."

"Call me Lynn. Get up, Trip, and come over here. Nice and slow, hands where we can see them."

He complied, nodding his enthusiasm. Even as one of the Ashlanders grabbed him, spun him around, and looped a rope around his wrists, he kept nodding, his face splitting into a hopeful smile. The Ashlander securing his hands laughed and said, "So what's up, Lynn, are you trying to start a collection or something?"

She rolled her eyes. "Fuckin apparently. At least I seem to end up with the compliant ones. I wonder how this one feels about gardening."

Trip laughed; it was a sound somewhere between amusement and hysteria. "Lynn, I'll . . . I'll feel however the fuck you want me to feel about whatever the fuck you want. Jesus. I . . . Thank you. Fucking thank you."

"Don't thank me yet, kid. You're still a fucking war criminal. But . . . say, did you merc that guy?"

"Yeah. Yeah, I fuckin did him right before he could do me."

Lynn looked back and forth between the holy terror in Trip's eyes and the rigid erection hanging out of the gutted signalman's trousers and muttered, "*Puta madre* . . . Jesus Christ, what is *with* these freaks?"

"Y'all, uh . . . y'all showed up just in time."

"Yeah, looks that way. Listen, kid, like I said last night, I can't make any promises about what your immediate future's gonna look like, but I did promise I'd help you out if you gave me something, and you sure as hell gave me something. Now let's get the hell outta werewolf country."

Trip laughed again, less manic this time. "I, uh . . . If I'm gonna be your willing POW, I do got one condition."

"Oh my God. What?"

"Y'all got food, right?"

**[AD 2261, 196 years post-War;
mid-December; Lexington, Kentucky]**

JULIA TOOK THE LITTLE SILVER MADONNA OUT OF HER rucksack and gave it a tender kiss on the forehead as she set it on top of the dresser on the far side of the bedroom, just behind the incense burner and next to the black taper candle, to the right of her books. Looking over the arrangement with a satisfied smile, she said, "There, right where You belong. Say, sugar, you, uh . . . you promise that this isn't weird, right?"

Magnolia, lounging on their bed nearby and counting the roofbeams, smiled and said, "Of course not, honey. This is your room, too."

"Okay. I, ah . . . I just don't wanna, like, intrude, y'know?"

"I promise it's not weird, hon. Tell you what: That can be the *goyische* half of the dresser."

Jules lit a cone of incense and muttered a quick prayer before walking over to the bed and flopping down next to Mags, where she stared up at the ceiling with her arms crossed behind her head. Mags looked her up and down, observing the map of tattoos and scars cris-crossing her arms, her long black hair spilling out around her head, the thoughtful look in her sad brown eyes, and asked, "Something on your mind, honey?"

"Eh, kinda."

"You wanna talk about it?"

"I dunno. I think I'm just having a little religious crisis. But I'm Catholic; those are normal for me."

"Well, I sure do know a thing or two about that."

Jules turned toward her and grunted. "Y'know, sugar, you and me have never, like, sat down and talked about religion before, but there's a couple things I've always wanted to ask you about."

"Yeah?"

"You're an atheist, right?"

"Sure am."

"Well, how does that . . . How does that, like, work?"

Mags sat up, flipped her long red hair out of her face, and fished a pack of cigarettes out of her pocket. She took a drag from one, handed it to Jules, lit another for herself, and said, "Yeah, I was wondering when that was gonna come up. Think about it like this. Do you think the people we spent all year fighting would've given two shits about how much faith I have?"

"Nah, sugar, I reckon they wouldn't."

"Exactly. So it's about loving myself for who I am, and loving my mama for who she is, and all the observances and whatnot are a giant 'fuck you' to the people who hate us. For me, whether or not God actually exists is neither here nor there. Listen, how much do you actually know about Judaism?"

"Not a lot, 'least not yet. Just what I've heard you and Mama talk about."

"Well, here's a fun fact. Most of our holidays commemorate attempted massacres."

"Yeah?"

"Yeah. The old joke is that Jews saying grace is 'They tried to kill us, they couldn't, let's eat.'"

"Huh. Y'know, I like that."

"Thought you might. Now talk to me, honey. What's on your mind?"

"I dunno. Everything around here is so . . . secular, I think is the right word. And it's great, we're better off that way, I love it here, but . . . y'know, the church was such a big part of everything when I was growing up that it's weird not to see it. I dunno where I stand with it, I guess; I'm a weed-smoking lesbian tranny and a reformed murderer cohabitating with my Jewish atheist girlfriend, for whatever that's worth, and I dunno if I still believe in God or not, and if I do then He's got a hell of a lot of shit to answer for, but I'm still thinkin about it."

"Sounds about right. Honey, can I say something that might or might not be fucked up?"

"By all means, sug."

"I'd kinda be surprised if you still believe in God after everything you've been through."

"Nah, yeah, that's a thought I've had a whole hell of a lot. But . . . y'know, Christmas is coming up in a couple of weeks. Doing Hanukkah with you and Mama was fuckin great, but do y'all have Christmas around here?"

"Not really. There's a midwinter festival, but that's pretty secular, like all the state holidays. To tell you the truth, hon, you're the first Catholic I've ever met."

"Huh. Y'know, sugar, I think I figured it out. It's not a religious crisis, it's a community crisis. I feel . . . lonely. I feel really fuckin lonely."

"Well, that's not so surprising. Moving here has been a huge change for you."

"That's an understatement. And like I said, I fuckin love it here, but . . . I think I could stand to be around other people like me."

"Like the Renegades?"

"Eh, not so much. I don't like the way those guys talk

about me; they wanna act like I did somethin special. I think . . . nah, I know; I know what I wanna do. I wanna have Christmas."

"That sounds like a good idea, hon."

"Really? That's not gonna be, like, weird or anything?"

"Well, as long as you're not expecting me to, like, participate."

"Ah, of course not, sug, I would never. But even so, there's no church around here—and thank God for that; fuck the church—but I'll still feel like a big idiot celebrating Christmas all by myself."

"We could bring your mom down here. I bet she'd love that."

"Ah, I don't wanna bother her. I know she and Kitty have gotta be real busy getting settled back in up there."

"It's your mom, you giant nerd. She'd love to hear that her daughter wants to spend the holidays with her. Plus, I really miss Kitty, and I know you do too."

"Yeah. Yeah, that I do. I'm glad Mom didn't have to go back to the old house all by herself, but this long-distance shit sucks. We should try and get 'em on the horn in the morning."

"We will, and you three can do all kinds of Catholic witchcraft and celebrate your god's birthday dancing around the Santa Tree or whatever it is y'all do."

Jules laughed, but she kept staring up at the ceiling, counting the white poplar roofbeams and the cracks in the daubing, the thoughtful, troubled look returning to her face. After another few minutes, she sighed and asked, "Sugar, do you think you could handle calling 'em up?"

"Yeah, for sure. How come?"

"I think I need to take a run."

"You sure that's a good idea, honey? It's the middle of the night and it's been snowing out there."

"I'll be careful. I just . . . I need to be alone for a while, clear my head and think about some stuff."

"Alright. Where were you thinking of going?"

She shrugged as she rose up from the bed. "Dunno. Figure I'll head down to Colby and let Lilly know I'll be away from the trees for a couple days, then just fuck off and see where I end up."

Mags sighed. "You promise you'll be careful?"

"I promise, sugar. I just need to think, is all."

Jules threw on a heavy flannel shirt and, over it, a sleeveless black button-up adorned with patches. Most prominent were the Ashlander state ecologist badge on the left breast and the word "RENEGADE" spread across the back in big block letters. She wrapped a scarf around her neck, picked up her rucksack, and the two of them walked out of their bedroom and into the kitchen, where Mags' mother sat reading a book by the wood stove. Emma looked up as the two girls walked in and asked, "Y'all goin somewhere?"

"I am," Jules said. "I've got a lot on my mind and I need to go think, so I'm goin on a run."

"'I'm goin on a run,' she says. It's the middle of the damn night, child."

"Yeah. That's the best time."

"*Feh.* You be careful, alright? You get yourself killed and break my daughter's heart, I'll kill you."

"I will, Mama. I promise."

Mags and Jules shared a long, warm hug and a slow kiss before parting ways. When Jules was gone, Mags sighed, pinched the bridge of her nose, and grumbled, "I fucking hate it when she does this."

"Reckon she needs it," Emma said, returning to her book.

"Yeah. Yeah, I know she does, and I'm not, like, mad or anything, I just . . . Mama, I worry about her."

"I know you do, child. But y'know she worries about you, too."

"Yeah. Yeah, she sure does. I just . . . I wish I could just give her what she needs."

"It don't work like that, Magnolia Jane."

"I know, I know. But sometimes I wish it did work like that. I just wanna help her quit hurting and give her the whole world."

"You already gave that woman a home, a family, a second chance at life, and a big stupid heart full of love. That's enough, child. Let her have her space. If it makes you feel better, y'know she worships the ground you walk on."

"Yeah?"

"She never fuckin shuts up. Every other word out of her

mouth is 'Mags is so beautiful, Mags is so sweet, Mags is so smart, I love her so much.' If you're worried about losing her, that ain't no concern. Let her breathe, child."

Mags' sour look curled up into a smile, and she said, "Yeah, Mama, I reckon you're right."

"I ain't never been wrong."

"Well, you were wrong that one time."

"*Feh.* And you ain't never gonna let me forget it, are you?"

"No, Mama, I ain't."

Emma glowered up at her, furrowing her brows, and grumbled, "*I have no son.*"

They laughed together, and Mags went to the stove to pour herself a cup of coffee and said, "Y'know, Mama, I may not be able to give Jules the whole world, but I know one thing I might can do."

"And what's that, Magnolia Jane?"

"I gotta go find my *shikse* a fucking Christmas present."

"*Feh.*"

Jules stepped out of the cabin and into a frigid Kentucky winter. There was an icy wind blowing down from the north, but it was a dry wind, and the sky above was bright with stars; perfect weather for riding. She wrapped her scarf around her face and headed around the side of the little cabin to the shed where she kept her most treasured possession: A sleek, black Triumph Bonneville T120 motorcycle. She smiled at the sight of it, as she always did, and grinned with anticipation as she walked it out to the road. The Bonnie was ancient, pre-War, and at that point every part of it had been replaced at least once, but she loved it like a child and so it ran like a dream. She mounted it, kicked it to life, and sat there finishing one last cigarette and watching the stars, savoring her solitude as she gave it a moment to warm up; New Lawrence, the farming town built on top of the ruins of Old Lexington, didn't have much of a night life, and save for a few lights in a few windows of the surrounding cabins, she felt perfectly alone.

Normally, Jules couldn't stand being alone. Being alone at night was when the demons came, and most of the time she felt like being around Mags, who she loved so much it hurt; or Emma, who had been so incredibly kind to her; or her comrades down at the forestry laboratory; or the friends she'd started making over the past few months were the only things keeping her sane. But now, her mind heavy with too many thoughts, the peace and quiet and solitude felt good. She thought that over as she puttered out onto the main road and opened up the throttle to head toward the 75; no longer being afraid to be alone meant progress, and hell, maybe there was such a thing as recovery after all.

As she headed out of town, past darkened fields and forests and not much other traffic, she did a few quick mental calculations and thought to herself: *More than two years since my last attempt. Over a year since I quit cutting. Can't remember when the last nightmare was, but it's been at least a couple of months. You're doin okay for yourself, Jules Binachi.*

She let the accelerator creep up and reveled in the feel of the engine rumbling between her legs and the dry, bitter wind whipping against her skin as she headed south. She laughed aloud with the joy of it all, letting the bike open up faster and faster, and she reached the Kentucky River and the turnoff to the agroforestry laboratory within just a few minutes.

The agroforestry laboratory was a few hundred acres of intentional woodland at the confluence of Boone Creek and the Kentucky River, and Jules saw it as her solace and salvation. To a casual passer-by in the dead of night, it would've looked indistinguishable from the other jumbles of field and forest that carpeted the New Lawrence canton, but even in the dark and driving past at speed she recognized every tree, every birdhouse, every bat box, every beehive. She slowed down to approach the cluster of prefab sheds and rammed-earth beehive huts near the riverbank and passed by a brake of saplings she'd been tending since early autumn, and she was half-tempted to stop on the side of the road and check on how her babies were handling the winter. But, of course, she'd already done that earlier that morning.

The facility was almost deserted so late at night, but as she rolled to a stop she spotted a young girl wrapped in a heavy winter coat sitting on the roof of one of the sheds, watching the stars. The girl stood up as she approached, waved down at her, and cried out, "Hi, Miss Julia!"

"Hey, Iris," Jules said, dismounting and walking over. "What the hell are you doing up there, kid?"

"I dunno."

"Fair enough. Is there any chance Lilly's still here?"

"Yeah, she's inside. She says she doesn't wanna walk home in the cold."

Iris climbed down the side of the shed like an acrobat and pranced ahead of Jules to the entrance of one of the beehive huts, where she threw open the door and announced, "Hey, Miss Lilly, Jules is here!"

Jules stepped inside to see a tall Black woman sitting beside a space heater with a cup of cider clutched in her gloved hands. She looked up with a quizzical expression and asked, "What are you doing back here, sweetheart? Did you forget something?"

"Nah. I wanted to let you know I'm gonna be out of town for a couple of days."

"Alright, baby. Is something wrong?"

"Nah, nah. Well . . . maybe. I need to take a little trip."

"Where to?"

"Dunno."

"Alright, supertramp. Are you sure that's a good idea? It's the middle of the damn night in December."

"I've just got a lot on my mind. I need to go clear my head."

Lilly rolled her eyes. "Sweetheart, talk to me. Come here, have a seat, tell me what you've got on your mind that makes you want to ride off into the mountains at asshole o'clock at night in the middle of winter."

Jules pulled up a chair beside her and they sat together in silence for a while before she sighed and said, "Lilly, let me ask you something. One of my new-girl-in-town questions."

"Whatcha got?"

"Do y'all got any priests around here?"

"The hell do you want a priest for?"

"Well, I wanna go apologize to God for existing." And she sighed again, pinched the bridge of her nose, and added, "I . . . I'm hurting, Lilly. And I know y'all know that, but, like, this ain't the kinda hurt that I wanna talk to my therapist about. I wanna go unload on somebody who . . . who *gets it*. If that makes any sense."

"You've got some sins in need of confessing?"

"Lilly, I have got *so many* sins in need of confessing."

"Listen, baby, you'd better not be trying to feel sorry for yourself again. You've put in a hell of a lot of hard work owning up to the person you used to be, and we're all proud of you, and you know wallowing in guilt never helped anybody. Not the people you hurt, and definitely not you."

"Nah, nah, it ain't like that. I feel . . . I feel lost, and I feel real lonesome, and I just need to take some time to think. So I'm goin on a run."

"Well, there's some churches around, but I guess that ain't the same. I wish I knew what to tell you, baby."

"Eh, I ain't expecting you to fix all my problems for me. I just didn't wanna disappear on you."

From across the room, Iris put her hands on her hips and said, "Y'know, Mags says that God is a lie made up by the ruling class to keep us in chains."

Lilly gave her an admonishing look, but Jules laughed and said, "Yeah, she sure does, and I reckon she might be right; she is the smartest person in the whole world, after all. C'mere, kid; I got something for you."

Iris came prancing over, and Jules dug around in her pockets until she found a small folding pocketknife and handed it over. Iris took it with a look of awe and reverence and said, "Oh, wow! Thanks!"

"I figure my favorite junior forester should have some of her own tools. You remember all that safety shit I taught you, right?"

"Duh. I'm not a little kid anymore, Jules."

"Of course, you're a responsible grown-ass adult woman. How old are you again, anyways?"

"I'm 12."

"You sure are."

Iris thanked her again before prancing back out into the darkness, and Jules leaned back in her chair and said, "God, I fuckin love that kid."

"She loves you, too," Lilly said, taking a long drink of her cider. "Y'know, she says she wants to be just like you when she grows up."

"Well, that's unfortunate."

"No, baby, it ain't. Think about that; you've turned into the kind of person that kids look up to."

"Huh. Yeah, I guess that is something."

"It sure is. Listen, baby, don't worry about the work. You take your time, and I hope you find what you're looking for."

"Thanks, boss lady."

"Don't you dare cuss me like that, Jules Binachi. I'm gonna tell Mags you called me the B Word."

They laughed as Jules got up to leave, and Lilly added, "Hold on, you're not taking that damn bike of yours, are you?"

"Of course I am. Only way to travel."

"Good Lord. Promise me you'll be careful, alright?"

"I will, Lilly. I promise."

"You checked your tires, tightened up the drive chain, all that?"

"Yeah, yeah. Say, Lilly, I got one more question."

"Whatcha got?"

"Where's nowhere? I'd like to strike out for nowhere."

"Well, Land's End is basically nowhere. You could head towards Hazard; it's beautiful this time of year. Head down towards Richmond and get on the 52."

"I just might. Say, did you ever get to meet my mom, or me and Mags's partner?"

"Can't say I had the pleasure."

"Well, they're gonna be in town roundabouts the 25th, I hope."

"Oh, a little Christmas get-together?"

"Something like that."

Lilly had been right. The mountains were beautiful by moonlight.

The road was sparsely traveled, and Jules was able to open up the throttle and eat up a lot of miles in just a few hours. She passed by Hazard and kept going to Matewan and the canton line, where a group of soldiers stood huddled around a burn barrel on the far side of the 1056 bridge. She rolled to a stop beside them as one of them reluctantly broke away from the group and came walking over. She fished a pass out of her pocket, handed it over, and said, "Mornin, bud. Sorry for the trouble."

"It's whatever," the soldier said, looking over the pass and handing it back with a yawn. "What's your business in Land's End?"

"Not much. Just felt like traveling."

"Cool. You ain't been on the road all night, have you?"

"I sure have, as a matter of fact. Is there a good place to stop around here?"

"Yeah, if you keep going and hang a right, there's a way

station on the edge of town. Food and beds and whatnot. Go fuckin get some rest, lady, the damn sun's about to come up."

"Yeah, that sounds like a plan."

The town was just beginning to stir to life as Jules rolled through its darkened streets and came to a stop at a tavern beside the railroad tracks. It was a humble little plywood structure with a crooked sign, nestled between a union hall and a fuel depot; it looked homey and inviting, and the morning crowd was only just beginning to roll in, which was nice, because even with her newfound good mood she didn't enjoy the prospect of walking into a building full of strangers.

The interior was smoky, dim, held only a few patrons huddled together in their own corners. She noticed a group of three in one corner wearing vests similar to hers; she gave them a wide berth as she walked up to the bar and took a seat.

The bartender, a Shawnee girl about her age, came walking over and said, "Hey there, stranger. You want some breakfast?"

"Nah, I been out on the road all night. I'd like a quick drink and a bed."

"Okey doke. Bunks are in the back; just gimme a holler when you're ready for one. What'll you take to drink?"

"Y'all got wine?"

"'Y'all got wine?' she asks. What kind?"

"Uh . . . the red kind?"

"Yeah. Be right up."

"Oh, and do y'all got pickles?"

"Of course we got pickles. What kinda barbarians you think we are?"

Jules fished around in her pocket and brought out a couple of loose rounds of .303 ammunition and set them on the bar. The bartender scooped them up and set down a tall glass of dark purple muscadine wine and a plate of three crisp, succulent pickles. She tore into one of the pickles, moaning with sublime satisfaction.

She glanced up and saw that the three other Renegades, two men and a girl, had noticed her and were walking over. She rolled her eyes and downed half of her glass.

"Uh, excuse me," one of them called out, "are you . . . are you Jules Binachi?"

"Last time I checked," Jules grumbled.

"Oh, wow. Well, ma'am, uh, it's an honor to finally meet you. I'd just love to shake your hand."

Jules held her right arm out, letting her hand hang limp like a dead fish. The two men seemed not to notice or care, each giving her an enthusiastic handshake before returning to their table. Their companion lingered, hanging back, and when they were gone she rolled her eyes and said, in a succulent baritone, "Miss Julia, I'm sorry about them two."

Jules looked her up and down. She had a familiar look in her sad green eyes, and she wore a long-sleeved flannel shirt under her cut, buttoned all the way up to her neck. The top of an angry black tattoo peeked out over her collar, and like-wise on her wrists. Jules smiled at her and asked, "So what's your name, renegade?"

"Oh, jeez. Uh, my name's Heather, Miss Julia."

"Sister, please call me Jules."

"Oh, jeez."

"Heather. That's a nice name."

"Thanks. I picked it out myself."

"Hell yeah. Listen, Heather, I been out on the road all fuckin night and I ain't got a lot of conversation in me, but . . . it's good to see you."

"Thanks. I told them two not to say anything, I figured you'd rather be left alone, but . . ."

"Nah, you're fine, sister. It's different when it's girls like us."

"Yeah. Yeah, if that ain't the fuckin truth. I'll, uh . . . I'll leave you be now. Sorry for the trouble."

"One sec."

Jules drew the sheath knife hanging from her belt and plucked one of the patches off of her vest, a square of denim with a semicolon embroidered on it. She handed it to Heather, who stared at it like fire from Heaven and muttered, "Oh my fucking God. Thanks."

"You take care of yourself, alright?"

"Yeah. Yeah, I sure will. Uh, you, too."

"Well, I'm trying."

She returned to her pickles as Heather walked off, and a

moment later the bartender returned, refilled her glass, and asked, "So what are you, some kinda bigshot?"

Jules rolled her eyes. "Un-fuckin-fortunately, yes."

"What's that mean, exactly? No offense, but, uh, I feel some kind of a way about serving a bigshot Renegade in my roadhouse."

"Ah, *non e niente*. No offense taken. I, uh . . . well, I co-founded the Renegades."

"Wait, are you--"

"Jules Binachi, yeah. Please, *please* don't try to tell me how brave and special I am. Tell you the truth, I'd feel better if you hated me."

"Didn't you, like, save the world, though?"

"Yeah, I finally decided to do one right thing after a life-time of fucking up. Don't us commies hate cults of heroism?"

The bartender nodded. "I do gotta ask, though. If you hate being a celebrity so much, how come you wear that vest?"

"Call it my scarlet letter. I ain't interested in lying about what I used to be. That's what the Renegades are, really; we're an accountability group."

"Huh. Y'know, that's pretty good."

"I like to think so. I just don't fuckin like getting special pats on the back for doing the bare minimum, is all."

"You saved the world, though."

"No the hell I did not. I was one small part of a team that

did that." She yawned. "Now, if you don't mind, I'd like to take you up on that bunk."

"Sure thing, sweetheart. You want somebody to come wake you up at lunchtime?"

"Nah. Just let me lie."

Jules slept hard and woke up just before sunset. She put her boots back on, shouldered her ruck, and crept out of a side door, hoping to avoid any evening crowds. It was colder than the night before, with frost on the ground and a light snow just beginning to fall, and the play of the dying light through the barren trees was beautiful. As she let the bike warm up, she thought about where she might go next, and she hit upon an idea.

"Oi," she barked at one of the strangers heading up to the tavern for an evening meal, "'scuse me, buddy, but would you happen to know how to get to Parson's Hollow from here?"

The stranger shrugged. "Ain't never heard of it. Sorry."

"It's over in Freeside. Ah . . . Would you happen to know how to get me at least as far as Charleston?"

"Oh, that ain't nuthin. You take the main road outta town thataway and then follow the river north till you get to the 119."

"Thanks, bud."

"No prob. Say, you're not thinkin of headin out now, are you? On that there motorbike?"

"Well, I was thinkin on it."

"Pretty steep country up thataway. You be real damn careful, alright, lady?"

"I sure will. Thanks again."

The weather grew pleasantly terrible as she headed north, relishing the frigid air and biting wind chapping every inch of her exposed flesh as the darkness drew in around her. She couldn't quite remember the maps of Land's End canton or the Freeside Special Economic Zone as much as she would've liked, but if she was right, then taking the Old 79 out of Charleston would get her close enough to Parson's Hollow and her friends by the time morning came. Assuming, of course, that the roads in Freeside were all passable, which was never a guarantee.

Land's End was even more thinly populated than New Lawrence, and she saw almost no other traffic, perhaps one bus or truck every few miles, and as she turned east to head deeper into the mountains she opened up the throttle and flew down the empty old highway, eating up miles as she whipped around corners through the hills, going steadily faster and faster. She knew she was going entirely too fast, given the weather and the terrain, but the speed was exhilarating and the danger prevented her from thinking; she could almost see her problems disappearing behind her along with the trees.

Around midnight, she passed by a herd of deer crossing the highway as the snow picked up and decided that, yeah, it was time to start being careful. She eased back on the throttle and let the bike start slowing down.

198 . . . 196 . . . 190 . . .

When she tapped the brake, she felt the bike start to vibrate and heard a faint rattling sound from somewhere below her. She fought back the instinct to squeeze the brakes too quickly and growled, "*Oh, you have got to be goddamn Jesus fucking Christ* fanculo la Virgine Maria *goddamn shit fucking kidding me . . .*"

160 . . . 155 . . . 140 . . .

The rattling grew louder, the shaking more pronounced, and amidst her stream of curses she muttered, "Come on, baby, come on, hold together, you're almost there . . ."

120 . . . 114 . . . 108 . . . 99 . . .

The drive chain gave way with a noise like a shotgun blast between her legs, and she just felt it kiss the back of her calf before it disappeared out into the darkness. She managed to keep the Bonnie upright as it coasted to a stop, then walked it off of the highway, cursing, kicking the pavement with the heels of her boots. She hadn't seen another traveler for over an hour, and the last settlement she'd passed was at least five or six miles ago, and she had no idea how far the next ahead might be. She had a spare chain and sprockets and a toolbox in her saddlebags, but the thought of trying to put it all together alone at night in the snow wasn't one she relished.

So, once she was safely off of the shoulder, she pulled the bedroll and tarp off of her rucksack and got to work building a fire.

"Miss Lilly said, 'Don't forget to check your drive chain, Julia,'" she grumbled as she worked. "And I said, 'Yeah, yeah, it'll be fine.' Jesus Christ, why am I so fucking stupid?"

Lilly's other admonishment—not to feel sorry for herself—repeated in her mind, and she swore and grumbled, "No, Lilly, it's true, I'm fuckin stupid. Would I be out here in the middle of the goddamn night about to sleep on the side of the fuckin road in the fuckin snow if I wasn't the stupidest goddamn woman who ever lived? Shit. Fuckin dumb as a sack of bricks, I am."

As she got her little fire going, it occurred to her that by rights she should've felt afraid to spend the night out in the open and vulnerable, but she didn't; this was the ACR, and shit like that just didn't happen in Ashland. Hell, if she tried to explain to an Ashlander why she might be afraid, they probably wouldn't know what she was talking about. And as she rubbed her hands together over her little fire, she sighed and whispered, "I don't fuckin deserve to be here."

The darkness didn't respond, so she continued: "You don't fuckin deserve any of this, you stupid Nazi trap."

She could almost feel Mags slap her on the back of the head as soon as the words left her mouth, but she was spiraling now, and she muttered, "You're a monster and you're a stupid faggot and you deserve everything they ever did to you."

Her right hand had wandered to the hilt of her knife of its own accord. Realizing what she was about to do, she stopped, grabbed her wrist, then drew the knife and rushed to tuck it away into the bottom of her rucksack, whispering, "Alright, Binachi, get it together, get it the fuck together. *Breathe, woman.* Now, what would Mags say? 'It wasn't your fault what they did to you,' she'd say. And she'd say, 'You don't gotta be the same person you used to be.' 'Keep doing the next right thing,' she'd say. Then she'd tell me she loves me and she'd tell me to quit bein dumb. Hell. If I can't do it for me, I can damn well do it for her."

And, to her surprise, the darkness answered her. A voice from the trees said, "Well, kid, she sure sounds nice."

"Alright, who the fuck is out there?" Jules growled as her eyes darted around.

A human figure emerged from the darkness, a gaunt, middle-aged woman wrapped in a long winter coat. She held her hands out and said, "It's just me, renegade, it's just ol' Molly. You need some help, stranger?"

Jules sighed, took a deep breath, tried to calm herself down. "Uh . . . I don't suppose you got a rear stand and an impact wrench in that coat, do ya?"

"Nah, but I got a warm place to spend the night if you're interested. My place is just through the trees there and I figured I should come check out all the commotion and cussing."

"Shit, I didn't wake you up, did I?"

"Nah, not at all. I'm usually up all night. Now stomp out that little campfire and I'll help you walk the bike over. You had supper yet?"

"Aw, hell. Thanks, lady. You said it's Molly?"

"Mmhmm."

"My name's Julia. You can call me Jules."

"I know who you are."

Jules started to roll her eyes, then stopped and said, "Hold up. You called me 'renegade' before you'd even had a look at me."

"Well, sister, Renegades are the only people who call themselves slurs when they're cussing the horror of it all."

"Oh, god*dammit*. I'm sorry."

"Don't worry about it, sister; I know how it is. Now let's get you in outta the cold, alright?"

As they walked the Triumph through the woods, Jules got a better look at Molly, and noticed the tattoos peeking out from her sleeves and covering the backs of her hands. As they approached a little plywood and turf shack nestled amongst the trees with the scent of wood smoke and food drifting out of it, she said, "Y'know, Molly, you're the second girl like me with ink like mine that I've met in the past 24 hours."

"Let's just say that it opened some doors when your story got around. Now go on inside and grab yourself a seat."

The little shack held a cot, a barrel stove, a table and two chairs, and a few shelves of dry goods, but what caught Jules' attention was the big wooden cross mounted on the far wall. She crossed herself as she headed toward one of the chairs and Molly came walking in behind her. The older woman loped over to the stove where a pot of soup was simmering, and she dished out two bowls, took the seat across from Jules, and said, "Talk to me, sister. You're running from something."

"Not quite. I mean, you ain't wrong, but it'd be closer to say I'm looking for something."

"Mmhmm. Any notion of what?"

"Not hardly. I just . . . aw, hell, if anybody would under-stand, I reckon you would."

"More'n likely."

"You mind if I smoke?"

"Go right ahead, kid."

Jules lit a cigarette, sighed, and said, "Molly, I fuckin hate myself. I hate myself for who I used to be and I hate myself for who and what I am, and the Ashlanders are all sweet as sugar and everybody wants to help me, but they don't . . . they don't fucking get it, do they?"

"Nah, they sure don't. I reckon you've already heard all the helpful words I've got to say a million times, so I'll just say this much: I know how you feel, kid."

"Fuck, it's good to hear that. That all has been on my

mind for, hell, my entire fuckin life, but y'know what it was that set me off the other day and sent me out here?"

"Tell me, sister."

"Well, Molly, it's almost Christmas. And I dunno if I still believe in God or not, and these days I'm leaning towards not, but . . ."

"You feel alone, and you feel like a fool doing penance without sacrament."

"Fuck, that's . . . that's it. You put it into words."

"I've always been pretty good at that. Hold on one sec; this here soup could use some garnish."

Molly got up and walked over to a cabinet beside the stove, and returned holding a loaf of bread on a platter, two tin cups, and a dusty bottle of wine. She wrestled the cork out of the bottle, poured them each a cup, and said, "Keep talking, sister. Tell ol' Molly what's on your mind."

"Ah, you're too good to me. Let's see . . . Well, I've always been the way I am, and I've always hated myself for it, but y'know what else? My girlfriend I was talking about when you showed up—she's Jewish, and she's like me. And some-times it feels like, y'know, I *must* be worth something if she thinks the girl I am now is worth keeping around, but . . . Every time Mags smiles at me is an act of grace I don't deserve. And I know guilt never helped anybody and wallowing in guilt is self-indulgent and useless, but I just . . . I don't know how to move on, y'know?"

"I sure do know. That's a real familiar story nowadays."

"Oh, yeah. And it being about Christmastime and all, y'know what I'd like? I wanna find a fucking priest."

"I figured you'd say that. Funny thing, Julia, that you haven't asked me what it was I did before I switched sides."

"I figure that's your business."

"You ain't exactly one for subtlety, are ya, kid?"

Jules glanced up at the cross on the wall, and down at the bread and wine on the table in front of her, and back up at Molly, who was smiling as though she'd just delivered the punchline to a joke, and she muttered, "Well, I'll be goddamned."

"I mean, not if we're lucky. I ain't been practicing since I disavowed the High Church during the war, and I reckon I been struggling just like you have, but, well, I'm here. If you think it'll help."

Jules was silent for a long, solemn moment, then looked up into Molly's eyes and muttered, "So . . . question."

"Yeah, kid?"

"What am I supposed to call you? I reckon you don't wanna be called 'Father' no more."

"My fucking name is Molly."

"Yeah. And . . . Molly, is any of this bullshit even real?"

"Let me answer that question with another question, Socratic-like. Does it matter?"

And Jules laughed, crossed herself, and said, "Bless me, Molly, for I have sinned. It has been . . . shit . . . about four, five years since my last confession."

"Lay it on me, kid."

"Well, before we get into all that . . . Molly, do I need to tell God I'm sorry for, y'know, the obvious things?"

"Of fuckin course not, kid. God made girls like us the way we are for the same reason loaves of bread don't grow on wheat stalks. And before you ask, I don't wanna hear you apologizing for being a girl who loves girls, either. And I'm gonna go out on a limb and tell you that you ain't gotta apologize for the ways other people hurt you."

"Alright, that shortens the list a bit. But I've done some bad shit, Molly. Some real bad shit."

"Tell me about it, kid. And don't hurt yourself; we've got all night."

"You absolutely sure? It ain't no fairytale."

Molly nodded. "Tell me your sins, my child."

The sun was just beginning to rise when Jules, with half a bottle of wine in her and with tears streaming down her cheeks, drew in a long, ragged breath and declared, "This . . . this is all I can remember. I am sorry for these and all my sins. Lord Jesus, Son of God, have mercy on me, a sinner."

Molly nodded and rested a hand on her shoulder. "That was some heavy shit, kid. You used to be one hell of a snake-eater, huh?"

"Yeah. Yeah, you might could say that."

"You have mortal sins on your soul and I can't offer you absolution without some serious penance."

"I mean, I figured as much."

"Yeah. Thanks for telling me all that; I know that couldn't have been easy."

"Yeah. Thanks for listening."

"You ready for your penance?"

"Fuck me up, *Madre*."

"You gotta keep doing the next right thing, kid. You spent the war fighting and bleeding for a better world, and that's a whole hell of a lot, and you should give yourself more credit for all that. But now it's time to build that better world. What do you do for work, Jules?"

"I'm a state ecologist—a forester. And I help take care of some kids and teach 'em about the trees and shit."

"That's a hell of a good place to start. How's this: All you gotta do is keep on doing those good works every single day for the rest of your life. Sound about right?"

"Well, Molly, that's what I was planning on doing anyways."

"Mmhmm. And you gotta go home and give your girlfriend a great big hug and a kiss and find a way to tell her how grateful you are without making it weird. And one more thing."

"Yeah?"

"Don't fucking drive a motorcycle through the mountains

in the winter in the middle of the goddamn night again, you fuckin idiot. Are you tryna get yourself killed?"

"Well, Molly, the answer to that question would be probably be yes."

"Fair enough. Julia, I absolve you of your sins in the name of the Father, and of the Son, and of the Holy Ghost. Now let's see what we can do about that drive chain and get you back on the road. Your girl's probably worried sick about you."

"Ah, you're too good to me. Say, do you got any way to travel yourself?"

"Nah. I been living that acetic-type life, tryna get right myself. There is a bus stop about a quarter mile up the road, though, if you're sayin what I think you're sayin."

"Reckon I am. If you ain't got any other plans, get yourself to the union hall over in New Lawrence on the 25th; we would just love to have you over for Christmas."

[*Later that evening; somewhere in the Freeside Special Economic Zone*]

The sun got to setting before 6:00 so late in the year, so when Tabby headed home for the evening and came upstairs she was expecting to find her roommate already awake and preparing for the day, but it was a surprise to find her perched atop one of the bedposts like a gargoyle, staring at the window as the sun's last deadly rays disappeared behind the mountains in the west. Becky was an odd roommate in a lot of ways, and her unique physiology was just one of them, but when Tabby had arrived at Professor J's clinic—which Becky described, affectionately, as "a halfway-house for sad bitches" — Becky had done her very best to be accommodating. After all, they understood each other's problems, and they did have one mutual friend.

As soon as the door opened, Becky gave a little wave and said, "Oh, hey there, roomie."

"Uh, hey, Becky," Tabby said, stepping inside. "Are you okay, hon?"

"Somebody's coming."

"Did you hear something?"

"Not yet. But my spidey senses are tingling."

"Is it, like, dangerous? Should we warn somebody?"

"Nah, they're coming out of the west. Probably a pal."

"Becky, people come and go through here all the time. What makes this special?"

"Dunno. But something's about to happen, I can feel it."

"Well, we'll find out when we find out, hon. Now please get down from there; you're creeping me out."

Becky lept up off of the bedpost and landed silently on the floor like a cat. "Oh. Sorry."

"And promise me you won't forget to eat tonight, okay? I don't really quite know how your whole situation works, but I know you haven't been eating enough. Y'know, I'm here if you can't find anybody else."

"I will, I promise. So how was your day, roomie?"

"Pretty good. We've almost got the machine shop back up and running. And . . . I feel okay, Becky. Honest to God. I can't remember the last time I felt okay before."

"Yee. You wanna talk?"

"Did you just say 'yee'?"

"Ugh, I keep forgetting that the future is a forsaken and godless place. I bet you don't even know what a lolcat is."

"A what?"

Becky started to reply, then perked up like a bird dog and rushed to the window, pressing her hands against it and muttering, "Oh, no fucking way."

"What is it? You hear something?"

"Tabby, this could be special."

"What is it?"

"Our mysterious stranger is on a motorcycle."

"Oh, shit. You think it's her?"

"Well, I haven't marked anybody else who drives a motorcycle."

Tabby walked up to Becky's side, and a moment later she heard the sound of a motorcycle engine coming down the road towards them through the rhododendrons and saw a lone figure approaching under the rising moon. Her face curled up into a wide, warm smile. Becky audibly squawked, threw open the window, and lept down two stories into the garden, sticking the landing and running around to the front of the building with inhuman speed. Tabby laughed and headed for the stairs.

Jules pulled up in front of the clinic to find a small, pale woman wearing ripped blue jeans and a t-shirt from some ancient band standing at the edge of the driveaway, waiting for her like a dog waiting for its owner. She looked to be about 20, but there was an intimidating sense of ancientness in her soulless black eyes.

When Jules rolled to a stop and hopped off of the bike, Becky ran into her at full speed, knocking her onto her ass, then drew her up into a bear hug, hoisting her several inches into the air. "Jesus fuckin Christ," Jules laughed, "I can't fuckin breathe! Some of us still need to breathe, y'know!"

Becky dropped her and kissed her cheeks. "Fuck, it is good to see you. I knew you were coming."

"Yeah, you were waiting for me on the front lawn. What are you, a golden retriever now?"

"Nah, still just a dracula."

"It's good to see you, too, you stupid bitch. How have you been?"

"Better. A lot better. How have *you* been?"

"Eh, some days are better than others. I feel pretty good tonight, though. So how's Tabby? How's the old man?"

"Our third alumna of the Sad Bitch Society should be joining us momentarily. She's hanging in there. I ain't no math magician, but given the circumstances I think she's doing pretty damn good."

"Well she probably doesn't have enough time in the day to be traumatized with you for a roommate."

"And what's that supposed to mean? I'll have you know that one out of one prison camp survivors think I'm an excellent roommate."

"Well, two out of two agree that you're an amazing friend. It's good as fuck to see you again, Becky. It really is."

They approached the front door of the clinic as four other people came walking out: A large, older Black man, two nurses, and Tabby, her brown curls bouncing as she broke into a run and threw her arms around Jules, showering her with kisses and stammering, "Oh my fucking god, Jules, how are you? How have you been?"

"Better now. Lots better now. Fuck, I missed you assholes."

"How long are you in town for?"

"Just tonight; I gotta get back to my girl. But I wanted to see all of you, and I've got somethin special to let y'all in on."

"Oh?"

She rubbed her hands together. "So . . . who wants to come to the Christmas party?"

The old man walked over and rested a hand on her shoulder. "That sounds wonderful, Julia. Who all else will be there?"

"Well right now it's just me, my mom, one of my partners,

my boss, and a mendicant preacher I met in the woods on the way here."

"I wouldn't miss it for the world. Now come inside; we were just about to have dinner."

"Hell yeah. Y'know, old man, I don't think I could ever thank you enough for everything you've done for me."

"Julia, allow me to express a sentiment with which I'm sure you are intimately familiar."

"Yeah?"

"Please don't lavish me with praise for doing the bare minimum."

"Yeah, maybe, but listen: It sure as fuck meant the world to me."

[Christmas eve; Lexington, Kentucky]

Mags and Emma came walking up to the union hall, the big clapboard barn just across the way from their cabin, late in the evening after the festivities had been ongoing for a while. A small woman with long, dark hair who'd been sitting on one of the benches outside having a cigarette saw them approach, gave an enthusiastic wave, and called out, "Oh, there's my bonus daughter! I didn't think you two would be joining us."

"Hi, Maria," Mags said with a smile. "I just wanted to pop in for a second to give Jules something. Plus I want to maximize the time I can spend with Kitty before y'all have to leave again.   Also, Jules still thinks I don't know what Christmas is, and that was kinda funny for a little while, but I don't like playing jokes on her."

"Oh, that's just lovely of you. Magnolia, come here and sit with me for a minute."

Mags and Emma took seats on the bench to either side of her. Mags balanced a box wrapped in brown paper on her bony knees and lit a cigarette, and Maria rested a hand on her knee and said, "I wanted to . . . I just wanted to thank you again, for everything you've done for my little girl. She's lucky to have found someone like you."

"Oh, I'm the lucky one. She's . . . Ah, you're her mom, you know how great she is."

"Maybe, but it's still nice to hear it."

Emma rolled her eyes and muttered, "Well, you ain't gotta live with 'em."

"I just love her so fucking much," Mags said. "She's incredible, and every day that I wake up next to her is the best day of my life. I . . . God, I've never felt so loved."

"And that's wonderful. Thank you, Magnolia, for taking such good care of my daughter. And now I suppose I'm lucky enough to have two."

"Fuck, are you trying to make me cry?"

"I'm only telling the truth. Now go on inside, dear. She'll be so happy to see you."

Mags gave her a kiss on the cheek before getting up to

head into the barn. The revelers were seated around one of the tables, talking and sharing a meal, and as she walked in Jules sprung up from her seat and said, "Oh, hey there, sugar. I didn't think you'd be joining us."

"I'm not," Mags said. "I just wanted to pop in for a second to give you this."

"You got me a Christmas present?"

"I thought it might be fun to participate in one of your culture's primitive rituals."

"Aw, sugar, you didn't have to do that."

"Open it, dummy."

Jules ripped the paper off of the package, opened the box, and stood staring at its contents for a long moment. As the moment dragged on into awkwardness, a person of indeterminate gender wearing a yellow sweater dress and a wide straw hat got up, walked over, and asked, "Well, what is it, sweetheart?"

"This is a jar of pickles," Jules said, pulling a jar of pickles out of the box.

Mags grinned. "What else do I get for the woman who has everything?"

"You fucking got me a jar of pickles for Christmas."

"I sure did."

Jules grinned, threw her arms around Mags, and declared, "Oh my fucking God, I love you so fucking much. You're perfect."

"You like it?"

"You're the best fucking girlfriend in the world and I love you so goddamn much."

Mags kissed the top of her head, turned to Kitty, and said, "Well, what are you waiting for? Get in here!"

"Yeah," Jules said, "us frail little ladies are gonna need a big, strong they/them to open this jar for us, y'know."

Emma and Maria stood watching them from the doorway as Kitty joined the embrace, and Maria smiled, sighed, and said, "Just look how happy our girls are."

"Mmhmm," Emma pontificated.

"Emma, I can't possibly thank you enough for everything your family has done for mine. I . . . just look at my baby, how happy she is."

"Well, she's done wonders for mine. You shoulda seen what a mess Magnolia Jane used to be."

"Emma, can I ask you a question? It's probably inappropriate and I'm still learning some things."

"Shoot."

"Do you ever miss your son?"

She scoffed. "Fuck no. My son was a weird little idiot and I've been blessed to be able to watch him grow up into such a fine young woman."

"That sounds about right. You know, I'm still not entirely sure what my Julia is going through, but I do know one thing, for absolutely certain."

"And what's that?"

"My son was never this happy."

NATALIE IRONSIDE was born in Vicksburg, Mississippi in the early 1990s and hopes that someday she may recover. Through a series of complicated misadventures and bad life choices, Natalie has been a soldier, a lumberman, a (former)

member of a cult, and a soils scientist in addition to being an award-winning author of speculative fiction. She is an active member of the Horror Writers Association and the IWW Freelance Journalists Union and currently resides in Florida where she lives surrounded by cats, houseplants, and guns and divides her time between writing, prowling by night, and bemoaning the horror of it all. She blogs regularly at https:// natalieironside.tumblr.com/, can be found on Twitter at @IronsideNatalie, and is trying her best.

9 798501 186156